SCATTERGUN SHOWDOWN

A rifle cracked somewhere to the north. Pettigrew, his boots clattering across the rocks, pulled up. Hoof beats coming his way. Moments later, men on horseback appeared on top of the draw, reined up, then came on.

The rider in the lead was wearing a silver star on his shirt. When they drew up, Pettigrew recognized the kid deputy from Canon City.

Pettigrew said nothing as four men dismounted in front of him. One was carrying the white sack with the money. Two thoughts went through Pettigrew's mind: It was over now, and the woman was safe.

Then suddenly his blood froze. He was looking into the big bore of a shotgun. One twitch of the man's fingers and his head would be blown off his shoulders.

A cruel ugly face was behind the gun. It said, "Well, now, looks like we hit the jackpot!"

ZEBRA'S HEADING WEST!

with GILES, LEGG, PARKINSON, LAKE, KAMMEN, and MANNING

KANSAS TRAIL   (3517, $3.50/$4.50)
by Hascal Giles

After the Civil War ruined his life, Bennett Kell threw in his lot with a
gang of thievin' guntoughs who rode the Texas-Kansas border. But there
was one thing he couldn't steal—fact was, Ada McKittridge had stolen his
heart.

GUNFIGHT IN MESCALITO   (3601, $3.50/$4.50)
by John Legg

Jubal Crockett was a young man with a bright future—until that Mescalito jury found him guilty of murder and sentenced him to hang. Jubal'd
been railroaded good and the only writ of habeus corpus was a stolen key
to the jailhouse door and a fast horse!

DRIFTER'S LUCK   (3396, $3.95/$4.95)
by Dan Parkinson

Byron Stillwell was a drifter who never went lookin' for trouble, but trouble always had a way of findin' him. Like the time he set that little fire up
near Kansas to head off a rogue herd owned by a cattle baron named
Dawes. Now Dawes figures Stillwell owes him something . . . at the least,
his life.

MOUNTAIN MAN'S VENGEANCE   (3619, $3.50/$4.50)
by Robert Lake

The high, rugged mountain made John Henry Trapp happy. But then a
pack of gunsels thundered across his land, burned his hut, and murdered
his squaw woman. Trapp hit the vengeance trail and ended up in jail. Now
he's back and how that mountain has changed!

BIG HORN HELLRIDERS   (3449, $3.50/$4.50)
by Robert Kammen

Wyoming was a tough land and toughness was required to tame it. Re-
porter Jim Haskins knew the Wyoming tinderbox was about to explode
but he didn't know he was about to be thrown smack-dab in the middle of
one of the bloodiest range wars ever.

TEXAS BLOOD KILL   (3577, $3.50/$4.50)
by Jason Manning

Ol' Ma Foley and her band of outlaw sons were cold killers and most folks
in Shelby County, Texas knew it. But Federal Marshal Jim Gantry was no
local lawman and he had his guns cocked and ready when he rode into
town with one of the Foley boys as his prisoner.

DOYLE TRENT

RAWHIDE RANSOM

ZEBRA BOOKS
KENSINGTON PUBLISHING CORP.

ZEBRA BOOKS

are published by

Kensington Publishing Corp.
475 Park Avenue South
New York, NY 10016

First Printing: December, 1992

Printed in the United States of America

Chapter One

He lay flat on his belly on a broken granite ledge high above the Arkansas River. They were firing at him from below, across the narrow gorge. From where they were they couldn't get him in their rifle sights, but if they kept throwing lead his way, a ricochet could eventually tear into him.

With a sickening "SPANG," a bullet bounced off the cliff over his head. Another clipped a branch off a twisted cedar growing out of the cliff. He heard the bullets hit a full two seconds before he heard the shots.

He couldn't raise up. Couldn't even look.

When he thought of it he knew he was lucky to have gotten to the ledge. They could have picked him off while he was climbing down to it — climbing down hand over hand in his stocking feet. Leather boots would have slipped on the crumbling granite. They had to have been watching, probably with field glasses. It was pure luck that he'd spotted them at the same time they'd spotted him.

What he had hoped to do by climbing down here was to get a look into some of the blind canyons that forked off the river gorge. He'd been on horseback on top, winding his way among the cedars, junipers, and cholla, trying to see down into the gorge. But from up there he couldn't see much. Couldn't see the bottom.

So he'd hobbled his sorrel horse, pulled off his boots and worked his way down to the ledge, using both hands at times to hang onto the boulders and cedars.

5

Now he was trapped.

A wry grin touched his sun-darkened face when it occurred to him that he had found their hideout. They had to be the bunch he was looking for, otherwise they wouldn't be shooting at him. If he could get back on top in fairly good health he could search for the route they had taken to get into the gorge—probably a horseback route. Before they spotted him, he'd seen two horses cropping the grass on a hill near the river. He'd seen two men, but suspected there were more beyond a bend in the canyon.

And a woman—if she was still alive.

Others had ridden into the canyons, looking for the woman, but there was a maze of side canyons, parallel canyons and pockets carved out by rain and the river over hundreds of thousands of years. Searchers could have ridden within two hundred yards of the men and their captive without seeing them. There was too much country down there. Wild, rocky, steep country.

A volley of rifle fire came from below. Lead slugs screamed into the rocks near his head and whistled off the cliff. Splinters from a rock stung his right shoulder. His right cheek took a numbing blow, and he knew he'd been hit by a ricochet. Blood from a cut on the cheek ran down his face and into his mouth.

All he could do was hug the ledge and make himself as small as possible.

Then the shooting stopped. He stayed still, trying to wait them out.

He could wait. They'd thrown everything they had at him, and he was cut and bleeding, but alive. It wasn't long until dark. While he waited, hugging the rocks, he could hear the river below, rushing downhill to Canon City and on to Pueblo. Crashing against the boulders. Eroding. Always eroding. He wondered what the men down there were doing. Moving camp? Probably. Now that they had been seen they'd move. Was the woman still alive? No way of knowing.

She was beautiful, so he'd been told. Long red hair

and a figure like a goddess, and twenty years younger than her husband. Beautiful and rich. Her husband, Charles B. Atkinson, was an investor in the Atchison, Topeka and Santa Fe Railroad Company, which had laid rails to Pueblo and on south to Trinidad.

He'd met Atkinson two days earlier in a plush hotel room in Pueblo. A chance at a five thousand dollars reward had drawn him there. It was early in the night. Atkinson had his plump body wrapped in a bathrobe, with pajama-clad legs sticking out the bottom. Deerskin slippers covered his feet.

"So you're Pettigrew," he'd said, his stern eyes going over Lemual Pettigrew from boots to wide-brim hat. What he saw was a thirty-year-old man about five eleven, slender, smooth-shaven with brown hair bunched around his ears. Grey eyes, straight nose, wide mouth and solid jaw. Not handsome, not homely, not tough-looking, not soft. Plain. Hard to describe. "What makes you think you can find my wife?"

Pettigrew had stood with his thumbs hooked inside his cartridge belt. He hadn't been invited to sit. The belt was pulled low on his right hip by a heavy single-action Colt in a worn leather holster. "Well sir, I've had some experience hunting men. And I'm a pretty good tracker."

"Hah," the older man snorted. "Pretty good? You'll have to be better than that. At least fifty men have been trying to track down my wife's kidnappers. Any idea where to start looking?"

"No sir. I was hoping you could give me a clue."

Atkinson's round face was always ruddy, and now was even ruddier. He clutched the lapels of his bathrobe and glared. "God damn it, man, if I had a clue I would have had it printed and distributed all over Colorado. I have no clue."

Pettigrew shifted his weight from one foot to the other. "Well sir, I've been told there is a note. The way I heard it it was written by your wife."

"Sure there's a God damned note. Every law officer in Southern Colorado has read it. But there is no clue."

7

"Can I see it, sir?"

Pale blue eyes grew speculative under thick grey eyebrows. Atkinson hesitated, then said, "You say you are a former Pinkerton agent and a former deputy sheriff. Why did you quit?"

"Personal reasons."

"Personal, huh? Responsible men don't generally quit a job without a conflict of some kind."

"I didn't quit a job, Mr. Atkinson. I finished the assignment I'd been given."

"Is that so." The thick eyebrows pulled together as Atkinson thought it over. He turned suddenly, opened a chiffonnier drawer and took out a soiled sheet of paper. "Handle it with care. And yes, that is my wife's penmanship. I'm certain of that."

Pettigrew read:

Charles. I am being forced to write this. I am being held against my will. I cannot say where. They want fifty thousand dollars. If it is not paid they will kill me. If it is paid they will let me go. They will contact you later. Please do as they say, Charles. I do not want to die.

Cynthia.

Looking up, Pettigrew asked, "As I understand it, this was found under the door of a waycar west of here."

"Yes. You know, everyone knows, we are building toward the river gorge. We intend to build a railroad through the gorge. One of our engineers found this when he opened the door to the waycar which he is using as an office."

"Nobody saw the man who left this note?"

"There was no one there that night."

"And the sheriff picked up some tracks leading west, then north, and lost the trail in the hills north of the river."

"That is so."

"Have they searched the canyons west of Canon City?"

"They have searched everywhere. Sheriff Bowen has some good trackers among his deputies and they lost the trail. What makes you think you can do better?"

Shaking his head, Pettigrew said, "All I can do is try, Mr. Atkinson. I've been told this note was found three days ago—have there been any more messages?"

"None." The shrewd eyes shifted down, then back to Pettigrew's face, somehow weaker.

"Surely," Pettigrew said, "they have given some directions—some instructions about where to leave the money."

"None."

"None at all?"

The round face was hard now. "I said none, and I mean none."

"I see." Pettigrew held his gaze. "Well, tell me this. Have your engineers found a route through the canyons? I mean a place to build a railroad?"

"Yes. We intend to follow the river. Of course, it will be quite a feat of engineering, but we have engineers who can build anywhere."

"So your men have been exploring the river gorge and the canyons over there?"

"Yes. But," Atkinson added quickly, "they have not been everywhere. They only looked for a possible route. It will take a great deal of blasting and digging, but a railroad will be built through the gorge."

Looking down at his scuffed boots, Pettigrew said, "I, uh, have tried to talk to Sheriff Bowen, but he wasn't much help. He said I was just one of many who would like to claim your reward. He wouldn't even deliver my note to you. I had to get the clerk downstairs to do that."

"True. Sheriff Bowen is constantly being pestered by fortune hunters. He did, however, verify your qualifications. I agreed to meet with you because of your experience as a detective."

"I appreciate it, Mr. Atkinson. I'll do the best I can."

That was only two nights ago, and already he'd found

them. Found them, sure, but not captured them. They weren't more than three hundred yards away as the crow flies, but twenty or more miles by foot or horseback. They'd move.

What he ought to do, he thought, was get back on top, ride like hell for Canon City and get the sheriff of Fremont County to round up a posse and keep a watch on the canyon country. He'd try to catch them when they came out, or at least pick up their trail. That would take a hell of a lot of men, but given enough time the sheriff could gather that many.

That was what he ought to do—but he wouldn't. He wanted the reward.

Atkinson had lied about not getting instructions from the kidnappers. Why had he lied?

Risking a move, Pettigrew felt his wound with his fingers. It was higher on his head than he'd thought, just under his hat, and it was sore to the touch. His fingers were sticky with drying blood, but the wound seemed to be only skin deep. He'd been hit by a fragment of a bullet or granite.

The move had brought no more gunfire. Did he dare raise his head and look down? He wanted to see as much of them as he could, see where their camp was, see which way they went when they left. Slowly, carefully, he raised his head, then ducked when he saw a puff of smoke come from a rifle barrel below. A second later the lead slug spanged off the cliff over his head. They intended to keep him down so he couldn't see anything. He'd gotten only a glimpse of a man in a slouchy black hat aiming a rifle.

They would move in the dark; so would he. Then what? It would take a lot of riding to pick up the trail where they came out of the canyons. A lot of riding and more luck. But for five thousand dollars, he'd try.

Come on, darkness.

Chapter Two

The longer he lay there, the harder the rocky ledge became. He wanted to look back, to fix the route to the top in his mind so he could find his way in the dark, but moving at all would be suicide. The man in the slouchy hat was watching from below, just hoping to get a shot at him. In his mind, he tried to picture the route.

Over thousands of years rain and snowmelt had eroded a narrow gulch down the cliff, and cedars grew out of the decomposed rock in the gulch. He had worked his way down by grabbing cedar roots, boulders and anything else he could. He'd even used his toes to grab holds in the rock. Now he had to go back in the dark.

"Well, hell," he muttered to himself, "it's either that or spend the night on this damn ledge."

Moving only his eyes, he looked across the gorge and up at the blue sky. Over there, on top of a sloping hogback ridge, stood a half-dozen cathedral-like sandstone spires. The spires had withstood the wind and rain while the granite had eroded away from them, and now they towered above the ridge like sentinels.

With some satisfaction he noticed that the sky was gradually turning darker. It had been a sunny day, and that was more luck. Afternoon thunderstorms were nothing unusual in August, and thunder and lightning made being on top of a hill, especially a granite hill, dangerous.

He risked another look down. The man with the rifle

was still there, a small figure. The rifle came up. Petti-grew ducked. The lead slug hit the cliff a few feet below him. The gunshot came right after it. They were waiting for dark too, and it was growing dark down there.

Now Pettigrew was in the shadows, but the sun was still shining on the east side of the canyon, turning the rocks dark shades of red and blue. The river below tumbled and splashed happily on its way. Again moving only his eyes, he saw the dark shadow line move slowly up the wall. Tiny specks of mica reflected the light like a thousand glittering eyes. It wouldn't be long now.

Again he raised his head, and this time it was dark down there. Too dark for the rifleman to see him? Better wait a few more minutes.

The next time he moved his head, he knew he was in the dark himself. Slowly he picked himself up. He could feel and almost hear his joints creak as he moved. "Lordy," he muttered. "I feel like a hundred-year-old man." The Colt sixgun hung heavy on his hip, so he unbuckled the cartridge belt and hung it around his neck, over his right shoulder. Then he reached for the first handhold.

With fingers like claws, he grabbed a cedar root and pulled himself off the ledge. His toes groped for something to get hold of. Grunting, sweating, his heart in his throat, he scratched, grabbed and scrambled. How damn far was it to the damn top, anyway?

He swore through his teeth when his fingers touched a cholla. "Damn, damn, damn." It was going to be fun pulling the cactus needles out of his hand in the dark. And he needed that hand. Needed three or four hands. But when he thought about it he figured he was near the top now. The cholla or cane cactus or whatever anybody wanted to call it didn't grow very far down into the canyon.

Then he was standing flat-footed instead of digging with his toes, and the cedar he had hold of was as high as his head. Maybe he could walk upright now. Carefully. The night was black, and he couldn't be sure where he was. When he took a step his foot slipped. Immediately, he dropped onto his belly, clawing for a handhold. He slid two feet and stopped. He crawled on his hands and knees, hoping he wouldn't meet any more cholla. He crawled until the ground felt level, then stood again, and walked carefully, a step at a time.

"Aw, dammit." His right leg collided with another cactus. Damn stuff was everywhere. Cactus needles were stuck in his pants leg like porcupine quills, and he knew from experience they would work their way through the duck material. Sure enough, they were soon digging into his skin below the knee. He was walking upright now, but every movement of his right leg was painful. Looking around him, he couldn't see more than ten feet in the dark. He'd left his boots under a horse-high boulder where he believed he could find them. But if he found them in the dark he'd have to run into that boulder by accident. He sure as hell couldn't see it.

He moved in the direction he believed the boulder to be, hands pushing cedar and juniper limbs out of his face, half-dragging his right foot. Both feet were sore now from walking in the rocks. But his sense of direction served him well. He found the boulder and his boots.

Lem Pettigrew was a long way from home, in the dark, afoot, with one hand and one leg full of cactus. Sitting under the boulder and working by feel, he pulled the needles out of his hand, then unbuttoned his pants and pulled them off. The needles sticking in his skin were easy to find. All he had to do was touch one and he knew immediately where it was. It took time, but he got them all out. The pants, though, were impossible. He pulled out what he could find and put his pants on, then took them off. There were too damn many, and they were invisible in the dark. No man could wear pants full of cholla needles.

So what're you gonna do, he asked himself. Sit here with your britches off and wait for daylight. No, by God. If he could find his horse he'd ride, britches or no britches. With his boots on, carrying his pants and gunbelt, he walked, stumbled and listened. An experienced horse could travel a long way with its forefeet hobbled, but the sorrel was a four-year-old gelding he'd only just taught to stand hobbled. It wouldn't have gone far. If it moved at all Pettigrew would hear it.

His senses served him again, and he heard an iron-shod hoof strike a rock. He moved in that direction, speaking softly. "Whoa, son. Whoa, Rowdy. It's me. It ain't a bear and it ain't a cougar, it's me." He couldn't see the horse, but he knew the horse, with its good night vision, could see him. "Whoa, partner," he said again.

It was a big dark shape. It could have been a tree or it could have been a boulder, but when it moved he sighed with relief. "Whoa, now."

Horseback, his gunbelt hanging from the saddle horn and his rolled-up pants on the fork of the saddle in front of him, he turned the horse downhill, heading for home. He depended on the horse's stronger senses to find their way out of the cedar hills and onto level ground. He chuckled to himself when he thought of how he would have looked in the daylight—wearing only a hat, shirt, shorts and boots. "I'm surprised you let me catch you, Rowdy," he said with a grin. "I wouldn't have let anything that looks like me come within a mile."

Staying on fairly level ground, winding between the sandstone and shale hills, he saw the dim lights of Canon City about midnight. His bare knees were sore from rubbing against the saddle, but, he said aloud, "They'll heal." He picked up the river on the south side of town, and was thankful for the darkness. "If anybody sees me they'll be haw-hawin' about this in the O.K. Saloon for the rest of the summer. Hell, even Betsy will make a joke out of it. Can't you walk any quieter, Rowdy?"

It was four more miles to his two-room cabin on the north bank of the Arkansas, just east of where Cripple Creek came down from the north and emptied into the river. The horse splashed across the creek, passed through a stand of old, rough-hided cottonwoods and stopped at the gate of the one corral.

Pettigrew was glad to get out of the saddle. His knees were very sore to the touch, now. He offsaddled the horse, threw the saddle over the top pole of the corral and walked with sore feet to the cabin. Inside he lit a lamp, sat on his wooden bunk and pulled off his boots. His stomach grumbled a reminder that he'd missed supper, but his answer to it was "Shut up." He lay back, covered himself with a wool blanket, and slept.

The sun was warming the sagebrush flats when Pettigrew awakened. He sat up, rubbed sleep out of his eyes, and stood. "Lordy," he grumbled. "Hope to hell I ain't out of flour and the damn bacon ain't spoiled. Wish I could afford to go to town and eat a woman-cooked meal. Wish I wasn't so damn broke."

He rummaged through a scarred and chipped chest of drawers until he found a clean pair of pants and shorts, and got dressed. "One of these damn days I'm gonna get me a bed with springs," he groused. Outside, he saddled Rowdy and went horse hunting. "Find 'em, partner. Sooner we run 'em in the sooner you can graze." He heard the bell on the bay mare clanging over east, and rode at a slow lope in that direction. With yells, whistles and a few pops from the end of his catch rope, he drove his six horses into the corral. He caught a rangy roan and turned the others out again. Rowdy ran and bucked with the pleasure of being free. The bell mare took a playful nip at a bay gelding's rump and dodged a half-hearted kick.

Pettigrew's log cabin held only what was necessary for living, and nothing else. A wooden table sat in the middle of the kitchen with two wooden chairs on opposite sides. The stove was a two-hole combination cookstove and space heater. A high, homemade bench held two water buckets and a tin wash basin. A few iron pots and skillets hung from nails on the wall behind the stove, and an empty coffee crate had been nailed to the wall for a cabinet.

The one other room held his bunk, a chest of drawers

and a wooden trunk. A long-barreled Winchester repeating rifle lay on top of the trunk. His clothes hung from nails. Outside, a galvanized wash tub hung on a log wall near the door. A three-sided loafing shed at one end of the corral was the nearest thing to a barn on the homestead.

Pettigrew washed his face, wiped it dry with a clean flour sack, and glanced at the raw spot on the side of his head. He fingered it gingerly. He sliced some bacon and mixed some flapjack batter. While he ate he tried to plan the day. What he ought to do, he knew, was to get on that blue roan and locate the few cattle he owned, see that they didn't wander plumb out of the territory. But what he decided to do was to keep on trying to earn that five thousand dollars reward. With that reward he could buy a mowing machine and put up some winter hay. Hell, he could do a lot of things.

He thought that they probably went north out of those canyons and up into the tall timber. No, if they expected to collect a ransom they wouldn't go too far from Pueblo—or maybe they would. Maybe they'd keep one or two men nearby to collect the money, while the rest hid in the high hills. One of the deputies had told him they'd picked up tracks of four horses. That would make it three men and the woman.

They were moving, staying in one place a day or two. That's what made it hard for the sheriff and his posse to find them. How were they moving that woman? They'd have to tie her on a horse. Must be hell on her. He wondered if she was still alive. She must be, otherwise they wouldn't have shot at him yesterday for getting too close.

All right, if they don't want to get more than a day's ride from Pueblo they came out of the canyons on the south and headed for the Sangre de Cristos. Or maybe they're still in the canyons. An army could hide in there. They'd move from where he'd seen them, but they had a hell of a lot of country to move in.

One of them had to communicate somehow with old Atkinson. They couldn't wring a ransom out of him

16

without communicating with him. That one could be with the bunch, or he could be in Pueblo. Hell, he could be in Canon City. He could be anywhere.

Just thinking of that possibility saved Pettigrew's life.

Chapter Three

He'd saddle the roan and ride west. Cross the river, cut over to the canyons and try to get lucky and pick up their trail. If he failed there, he'd head north and see if they came out where the river went into the canyons. Lordy, he thought, shaking his head. It would take at least three days riding to search every place they could come out. And if they didn't come out it would take several days to search the canyons. By that time they would have collected the money and either turned the woman loose or killed her.

They knew the canyon country. They knew where they could get in and where they could get out, and they knew where to hide. They had a lookout who could see anyone coming long before anyone saw him. If he spotted anyone coming their way, they'd move. That was how they'd stayed out of sight of the sheriff and his posse. But the sheriff should have cut their sign. Did somebody lead the posse in there? Could be. The sheriff could have got help from some sourdough who knew the country, and he could have led the posse away from any sign. If that was so, he was in cahoots with the kidnappers.

And—the thought came to Pettigrew suddenly—somebody among them was known in Canon City, and it was possible he recognized Pettigrew. They probably had field glasses. No doubt they did. They could have focused on him and recognized him. They knew Lemual Pettigrew was trying to earn that reward.

They might try to stop him.

With a bullet.

That's why, when he walked out to the corral, his eyes were searching the cottonwoods, the tall weeds and brush that grew along Cripple Creek. That's why a small movement in the weeds caused him to turn suddenly and run back to the cabin. It occurred to him as he ran the dozen long steps that it could have been a calf or a coyote or anything but a man. Just the same he yanked the door open and dove inside headfirst, picking up a splinter from the floorboards.

That's why the rifle bullet zinged harmlessly over him and thunked into the far wall.

Pettigrew rolled out of the doorway, pulled a splinter from the palm of his left hand, and hurried to the bedroom and the lever-action rifle on top of the wooden trunk. Quickly he jacked a bottle-necked .45-.75 cartridge into the firing chamber and walked with fast steps back to the kitchen. He ran the two steps it took to get past the open door.

There were two windows in the cabin, one in the kitchen on the south side facing the river and the other in the bedroom facing north. Wire screens had been nailed across the windows to keep flies and mosquitos out. The shooter was over by the creek. Pettigrew yanked off his hat and squatted under the kitchen window. Fear had his stomach knotted and made his hands tremble. How many were over there? If he showed himself in this window one of them could sneak around back and shoot at him through the other window. He'd have to watch both.

Trying to stop his hands from trembling, Pettigrew slowly raised up to where he could see out with one eye. At first he saw nothing, then a small movement in the weeds. Slowly, he raised the rifle and waited. The movement became a blue shirt and a dark hat. Pettigrew snapped a shot, but knew he'd missed.

Ducking immediately, he muttered. "Dammit, what's the matter with you, Lem Pettigrew. You've been shot at before. You've been shot at and you've shot back. Hell,

19

you killed a man once. Stop shaking like a coward and do something—but don't be fool enough to run out there and make a target of yourself."

Before he could shoot with any accuracy out the window he'd have to tear the screen loose, or shoot out the door. The window was a better port hole. With the butt of the rifle he knocked one side of the screen loose, and took another look. Seeing no one, he poked the barrel past the torn screen, aimed at the spot where he'd last seen the man and squeezed off a round. The exploding cartridge sounded like a cannon inside the cabin. Quickly, he jacked another round into the firing chamber and watched.

He got only a glimpse of the shooter before he ducked back. A lead slug tore a small hole in the screen and thudded into the wall. Another shot followed that. The shooter was behind a big tree; Pettigrew had seen that much. "You son of a bitch," Pettigrew muttered. "Caused me to ruin a window screen, trying to kill me. You son of a bitch."

Fear was forgotten now, as Pettigrew looked out again, saw a shoulder and arm behind the tree, aimed and fired. The Winchester bellowed, and acrid gunsmoke burned Pettigrew's nose. The shoulder and arm disappeared, then reappeared for a second.

"Dammit, I thought I could shoot better than that." When he looked again, only an eye and half a face showed behind the tree. "Come out of there, you bastard."

It was a standoff. It would take damned good shooting or a lucky shot for either man to hit his target. But the other man could leave. He had to have a horse back in the cottonwoods somewhere. Pettigrew couldn't leave.

Unless he went out the other window.

He snapped another shot, saw splinters fly off the side of the tree, then hurried to the bedroom. The country back of the cabin was mostly flat, dotted with sagebrush, cane cactus and juniper. Only an Indian could hide out there. But Pettigrew took a long look anyway before

20

knocking the screen loose and crawling out headfirst.

He hit the ground on his hands, but hung onto the rifle, then stood, bending low. Another careful look around, and he made his way to the west end of the cabin. Peering around the edge of the log wall, Pettigrew exposed nothing more than his right eye and the side of his face. He spotted the man, still behind the tree. As he watched, the man put a rifle to his shoulder, squinted down the barrel and fired another shot through the kitchen window. He didn't see Pettigrew.

"Damn fool," Pettigrew muttered. "A gunfighter you ain't." He raised his rifle, aimed and fired.

The man suddenly dropped the gun, spun half-around, clutched the right side of his chest and fell onto his knees in the weeds. Pettigrew ran, ran right at him, carrying the Winchester in his left hand and drawing his sixgun with his right. He was nearly on top of him before a scary thought entered his mind: there might be another shooter. If there was, Pettigrew was a perfect target.

And Pettigrew would be the damned fool.

He jumped behind the same tree, but kept the downed man covered with his sixgun. Looking around wildly, he saw a horse tied to a tree limb near the creek, but nothing else.

"Who are you?" he said. "Who's with you?"

The wounded man was still on his knees. He half-turned and sat on the seat of his pants. Blood was spurting from the right side of his chest, covering the front of his shirt. His face — a middle-aged, thin, beard-stubbled face — was twisted in pain. Pettigrew stepped over in front of him, squatted and put the bore of the sixgun only inches from the end of his nose. "Who are you? Who in hell are you?"

Through clenched teeth, the man said, "Go to hell."

"I've seen you before. In the O.K. Saloon. Why the humped-up hell were you trying to kill me?"

"I ain't tellin' you a God damned thing."

Pettigrew stood, lifted a heavy pistol out of a holster on the man's right hip, and picked up the dropped rifle. He

21

had his left hand full with two rifles and a pistol. "All right, stay here and bleed to death. I'll just take your horse." He turned toward the tied horse.

"You ain't . . ." a shudder ran through the man ". . . you ain't gonna leave me here?"

"Naw, I'll go get the sheriff. He'll haul your carcass to town in a wagon. Maybe somebody'll pay for a funeral."

A long groan came out of the man. "You ain't — you cain't just leave me."

Pettigrew turned, walked back and again stood in front of the man. "Hell, mister, you tried to kill me. I've seen you before but I don't know you. You've got nothing against me. Go ahead and die, you son of a bitch."

"Shit, I'm bleedin' like a stuck hog. Git me to a doctor." The mouth twisted in pain. "Listen, I . . . I know somethin' you wanta know."

"What?" Pettigrew squatted again. "Do you know where Mrs. Atkinson is?"

"I ain't tellin' you nothin'."

Standing, Pettigrew said, "Die, then."

"I ain't tellin' you nothin' less you get me to town."

"All right. I've got a team and a spring wagon. Suppose I haul you to town, to a doctor, then what would you tell me?"

"God damn, man, I'm bleedin' to death." He grunted with pain. "I know about that woman."

"Is she alive?"

"Yeah. She's . . . God damn, man."

"All right. It'll take a while. I'll have to run the horses in and harness the team."

"Hurry up. I'm dyin'."

Pettigrew hurried. He used the downed man's horse to wrangle in his own horses, threw a harness on a bay and a sorrel, a pair that he could work in harness or under a saddle, and hitched them to a light spring wagon. Back at the cottonwoods, he found the man stretched out on his back, breathing heavily, eyes squinted tight.

Kneeling beside him, Pettigrew said, "I don't think you're gonna make it, mister. Tell me about Mrs. Atkin-

22

son."

The eyes half-opened. "She's . . . she's all right." He tried to raise up, fell back. "Help me."

Pettigrew tried. He got an arm under the man's shoulders and another under the knees. With a groan, he straightened, carrying the man. Staggering under the weight, he carried him to the wagon, layed him in the back. Climbing up onto the seat, he gathered the driving lines. "If I run the team it'll be a rough ride, if I don't you might die before we get to town."

There was no answer. Pettigrew looked back. The stubbled face was relaxed. The eyes were half-open, staring blankly.

"Aw hell," he spat. He retied the lines to the brake handle, climbed over the seat, squatted. "Well what the hell do I do now?"

He tried to think. He'd have to tell Watson, the sheriff of Fremont Country, Jack Watson. A hard man. Hell on noisy drunks. Suspicious of everyone. He'd be suspicious of Lem Pettigrew, hauling a dead man to town, saying the man tried to kill him. How could Pettigrew prove it? Show the sheriff some bullet holes? Why, the sheriff would ask, was this jasper trying to kill you?

Pettigrew knew why. This was one of the kidnappers. He'd recognized Pettigrew yesterday in the canyon, and believed he was too close to their hideout. This morning he'd tried to put Pettigrew out of the way.

But Pettigrew couldn't tell the sheriff that. If he did, the sheriff would round up a posse and search the canyons again. The posse might get lucky.

He knew he ought to tell the sheriff, for the woman's sake. Yeah, that's what he ought to do. But the woman was all right. This jasper had said so. Another day or two wouldn't matter.

That's what Pettigrew tried to convince himself. After all, he'd spent a miserable day on a high rocky ledge dodging bullets, and he'd been shot at again this morning. All because he was trying to rescue Mrs. Atkinson. He had a right to try for that reward.

Sure. He searched the dead man's pants pockets and found a worn leather wallet. The wallet held a ten-dollar bill and three ones. Maybe, he thought, this would pay for a decent burial. He put the money back. It was in a shirt pocket that he found a letter. The letter was in a folded envelope addressed to Mr. Charles B. Atkinson, written by a woman. It was sealed, and had enough postage on it to send it around the world. Pettigrew wanted to read the letter. He knew he shouldn't. He knew he would.

Digging a folding knife out of his left pants pocket, he started to slit the envelope, stopped. Sheriff Watson would know he'd opened the envelope. How could he explain that?

"Well hell." He slit the envelope, took out a one-page letter, and unfolded it.

Chapter Four

It was Mrs. Atkinson's handwriting.

Charles. I am afraid for my life. They are treating me terribly. Please put fifty thousand dollars in a white flour sack. Go west to the end of the railroad, then cross the river and go five miles south. Tie the sack to a sage bush. Please come alone. They ordered me to warn you not to notify the officers of the law. This is the second and last warning. Do not make the mistake you made the first time. They will be watching, and if they see anyone else they will kill me. Do this on Thursday morning soon after the sun rises. Please Charles, do everything they want and free me from these terrible men. I cannot stand this treatment much longer.

Cynthia.

"Huh," Pettigrew grunted. Squatting on his heels in the back of the wagon beside a dead man, he ran it all through his mind. This gent was heading for Pueblo to mail this letter. The post office in Pueblo was busy enough that he could have dropped it in the outgoing basket or whatever they used there without being noticed. It would be delivered to Charles B. Atkinson later today, tomorrow morning at the latest.

And this gent intended to eliminate Lem Pettigrew on his way to Pueblo. He should have given up when his first shot missed. He should have climbed on his horse and high-tailed it. He was no soldier. What was he? His boots were the flat-heeled kind that miners wore, and they'd seen plenty of wear. His pants were the riveted denim

25

kind, now a favorite of the miners and farmers, held up with leather suspenders. His guns, well, the sixshooter was old, but the rifle was almost new.

Looking at the face, Pettigrew was surprised at how innocent and peaceful it seemed to be. It had survived a lot of weather and seen a lot of hard times, but now it looked to be as innocent as a sleeping child. This man was one of the prospectors who'd combed the canyons, attracted by the streaks of minerals in the granite. That's why he knew the canyon country. He probably was the one who led the sheriff's posse away from the kidnappers. Because he was known in these parts, he would attract no attention.

This man was also a killer — or at least he'd intended to be.

Pettigrew wished now he'd left him in the weeds. Oh, well, maybe it made no difference. He could show Sheriff Watson where the man had fallen. There was plenty of blood. Only one thing to do now. He climbed back onto the wagon seat, gathered the lines and clucked to the team.

Turned out the sheriff was out of town. The only deputy in the sheriff's combination office and jail was a green kid. Well, Deputy Ellsworth had to have been twenty-one, but he looked and acted like a teenager, and everyone referred to him as "that kid deputy."

Pettigrew attracted attention as he drove down the broad dirt street with a dead man in the back of his wagon. By the time he halted the team in front of the sign that read "Sheriff, Fremont County," there were a half-dozen men following to see what happened. And fifteen or twenty kids. The men and women of Canon City had no entertainment except making babies, and kids were everywhere. They yelled at each other to "C'mere, 'mere quick! Hurryup!" They came, boys in worn and torn britches, ragged hats and caps and sun-bleached hair, girls in torn and dirty dresses.

But they didn't touch anything. Instead, they stood back and stared in quiet awe.

26

A man in laborer's clothes said, "Now you kids stay back." To Pettigrew he asked, "What happened, mister?"

"I'll have to tell the sheriff," Pettigrew said. "Hold my team, will you."

But all he got was Deputy Ellsworth. The deputy adjusted his gunbelt and holster, got it hanging just right, tilted his nearly-new Stetson a little to one side, and stepped out into the crowd. "Stand back there—ever'body stand back now." He was slender, smooth-shaven, smelling of bay rum. "It's my duty to see what's goin' on here." He viewed the body, picked up one arm, tried to feel a pulse, and announced, "This man's dead." Facing Pettigrew, he said, "I've seen you around town before. Did you shoot 'im?"

Pettigrew stood with his thumbs inside his gunbelt. "I had to, or get shot myself."

"Hmm." Deputy Ellsworth looked hard at Pettigrew. "You better have a good story."

"He tried to bushwhack me at my cabin. I outshot him. That's as much as I know about it."

"Hmm."

Pettigrew waited to see what the deputy would do next. He wished the deputy would ask another question, an important one. Finally, he turned to the crowd himself, "Does anybody recognize this man?"

"I'll ask the questions," Deputy Ellsworth said.

"Name's Muley. That's the onliest name I ever heered 'im called." The speaker was a short man in bib overalls, a grey beard and a bill cap.

"Do you know anything about him?"

"Now listen here, I'm in charge until Sheriff Watson gets back."

"I seen 'im in the O.K. a bunch of times. I heered he was a diggin' for color in them canyons over yonder. They said he allus rode a mule, but the mule died."

"Do you know if he ever did any work for the sheriff? I mean, like helping hunt for Mrs. Atkinson in the canyons?"

Another man stepped up. "Yup—that's him. He

knowed them canyons, and he volunteered to lead us in there. Didn't find any sign of 'er, howsomeever."

"You were with the posse that went in there?"

"Yup. A feller c'd get lost in there. You say he tried to kill yu?"

"Yeah. He shot at me from the brush along Cripple Creek. Don't ask me why, 'cause I don't know. Have you seen him around town lately?"

"Naw. Cain't say I have."

"Now listen, I'm in charge here." The deputy tried again to take charge of the situation.

"Did he seem like a dangerous man, a dishonest man?"

"I dunno. Kept to hisself most of the time. Seen 'im talkin' to some hardcases a while back. They was off to theirselfs like they didn't want nobody to hear what they was sayin'."

"Well . . ." Pettigrew looked at the sky, saw the sun nearing its peak, then turned to the deputy. "What should I do with him?"

"We ain't got no undertaker," someone said. "Only Doc Allison knows anything about dead folks."

"He's got a shed he keeps the dead 'uns in 'til they're buried."

"I know where it is," Pettigrew said. "I'll haul this carcass over there." To the deputy he said, "When the sheriff gets back, tell him I'll be at my homestead the rest of the day."

"You ain't leavin' yet. Not 'til I say so."

Climbing onto the wagon seat, Pettigrew gathered the driving lines and clucked to the horses. The crowd followed him the two blocks to a one-room shed, once used as a wood shed, across the alley from the doctor's office.

"The doc ain't here," a man allowed. "I seen 'im a leavin' town this mornin' in his buggy."

Three men helped Pettigrew carry the dead man inside and lay him on a canvas cot. One took a wool blanket from a hook on a wall and covered the body. "Keeps the flies off," he said.

"Got to bury 'im purty quick," another allowed. "Hot

as it is, he's gonna start stinkin'."

Outside, Pettigrew again climbed onto the wagon seat. "Tell the sheriff I'll be at home."

"Wait a minute. Just you wait a damn minute, now. I'm takin' a written statement from you."

Looking down at the deputy, Pettigrew drawled, "I'll give my statement to the sheriff. If I was you I'd ask questions and find out all I could about this gent. Sheriff Watson would appreciate that."

"You're not tellin' me what to do." All of a sudden the kid deputy was snarling like a cornered coyote. Pure venom showed in his eyes. "No God damncowpuncher tells me what to do."

It gave Pettigrew pause. This kid could haul out that shooting iron and blast away. Maybe it would be best to do as he said. Aw hell—Pettigrew didn't want to spend the next hour answering questions. He'd have to do it again when the sheriff got back. Finally, trying to sound unconcerned, Pettigrew said, "Naw." He clucked to the team. "Naw, I'm not telling you what to do." The hair on the back of his neck bristled as he drove away. Not until he'd gone a block and a half did he let his breath out.

Every time he passed the combination post office and stage stop, Pettigrew wondered whether Betsy would come to the door and wave to him. When she did, he stopped and talked. This time he didn't want to talk. But this time she not only waved, she called his name.

"Oh, Lemual. Lemual." She was waving a letter, standing in the door in an ankle-length dress, her light brown hair combed back and tied with a red ribbon behind her head. She was slim, with wide brown eyes. Pretty.

Pettigrew reined in the horses, and she ran out to him, holding the letter in one hand and holding her long skirt out of the way with the other. "It's for you, Lemual." She handed it up to him. "I don't believe you ever got a letter before."

He had to grin down at her upturned face. "You're right, I don't get much mail. You sure it's for me?" The

29

letter had his name on it and Canyon City, Colorado, with the name of the city misspelled. It had been written with a lead pencil. There was no return address.

"Are you all right, Lemual? What was the crowd for at the sheriff's office?"

"I think I'm fine, Betsy. I . . . uh — a man took a shot at me this morning and I shot back. He missed. I didn't."

The pretty face suddenly tightened. "Why? Why would anyone shoot at you? You haven't had any fights with anyone."

"I don't know. I'm hoping the sheriff can figure it out when he gets back."

"You haven't been to town much lately. Is anything wrong?"

"No, I've been busy, is all."

"Do you suppose that when you come to town you could stop by and say hello?"

Grinning again, he allowed, "That's about the only reason I ever come to town, Betsy."

"I'll fix you some supper anytime."

"That makes two reasons. I'll be back in a few days."

"Can I count on that?"

"You can bet the ranch on it."

She stepped back away from the wheels. "Take care of yourself, Lemual."

"It's Lem, remember? Only my mother called me Lemual."

She smiled broadly. Slightly overlapped upper teeth didn't spoil a pretty smile. "Okay, Lem."

On his way back, Pettigrew forgot about the dead man. Betsy was on his mind. Betsy was a widow. Her husband Anton Buhler had been a sawyer at the Canon sawmill. He was careless for only half a second, but that was all it took to lose his right hand. There was no doctor anywhere near Canon City then, and he bled to death. That was over two years ago. Betsy had grown up in a large family headed by her father, a barber who didn't make much money, and she knew how to stretch a dollar. She lived alone in a one-room clapboard cabin two blocks from the post office where she worked as an assistant to the postmaster.

Young men were plentiful, and they all tried their charms on Betsy. Some had honorable intentions; others intended only to get under her skirts, give her something she was used to, being a widow.

She discouraged them all except Lem Pettigrew. There was something about him she liked. He didn't know what.

"Hell," he thought glumly as the wagon rattled out of town, "Sometimes I don't even like myself."

Somehow that reminded him of the letter. Sitting on the driving lines to free his hands, he let the horses take their time on the wagon road which paralleled the river. For the second time that day he slit open an envelope, unfolded a sheet of paper and read. Before he read the lead-penciled message he read the name at the bottom and groaned.

Hello Lem old partner. Bet you are some surprised to hear from me. I heard you quit the Pinks and bought some homesteads on the Arkansaw and I hope this letter gets to you. They will be lettin' me out of here soon for what they call good behavior or something like that. Who do you think I will want to see when I get out. You bet your bloomers. We have got to have a meetin. Do not look for me. I will find you. Signed John Beans Gipson your old pardner. Or maybe I should say ex-pardner.

In his mind, Pettigrew could see Beans Gipson and hear him speak the words in the letter. He spoke "old partner" with a lot of sarcasm.

A long sigh came out of Pettigrew. Shaking his head sadly, he refolded the letter and put it back in the envelope.

"Just what I need," he grumbled.

Chapter Five

Sheriff Jack Watson was six-two, gaunt, with high cheekbones and hollow cheeks. A grey walrus moustache made his mouth look permanently downturned. He studied Pettigrew with faded suspicious eyes. "I believe you're tellin' the truth." He fingered the empty .44-.40 cartridge casings he'd picked up. "But you ain't tellin' me everything."

Pettigrew had showed him the bloody weeds, the cottonwood with a bullet crease, the bullet holes in his cabin wall. "Like what?"

"Like why. He mad at you for something?"

Shaking his head, Pettigrew said, "Not that I know of. I've seen him in town, but I've never had any words with him."

"I found that letter in his pocket." The voice was accusing, "The one you opened and read."

"Does that tell you anything?"

"Makes me wonder why you just had to read it."

"Well." They were standing near the sheriff's brown horse tied to a corral post. "Wouldn't you be curious if somebody tried to kill you? Wouldn't you go through his pockets?"

"If I was you I'd leave a personal letter for an officer of the law to read."

Pettigrew shrugged. "I should have, I reckon, but I was curious."

"So now you know about the ransom note."

"Yeah."

"Which makes me wonder if you know something about the kidnapping, something that'd make Muley Reece want to shut you up."

"It makes me wonder if Muley Reece was one of the kidnappers. Someone told me he led you and your posse into those canyons over west."

The suspicious eyes narrowed. "What do you know about the kidnapping? Did you see something? You trying to get the reward all by yourself?"

Here it was. Pettigrew had to tell everything or lie. He studied his boots, squinted at the eastern horizon. "Sure. I could use the money."

"What'd you see?"

Pettigrew hesitated, trying to think fast. If he told all, the sheriff would gather another posse and go back to the canyons. Then, maybe not. Maybe he'd . . . what was the use lying? "I got close to them yesterday on the west rim of the canyons. Too close. They were down in the bottom where I couldn't see them good enough to recognize anybody. I didn't see the woman. But it was them. They shot at me."

Now Sheriff Watson was squinting at the horizon. "That explains it. We'll have to go back in there and ride every inch of that country."

"They won't be there."

The eyes bored into Pettigrew's face. "You sure about that?"

Shrugging, Pettigrew said, "I'm only guessing. You read the ransom note. Your guess is as good as mine."

Dropping his gaze, Sheriff Watson said, "Yeah, you're prob'ly right."

"Are you gonna deliver that note to Mr. Atkinson?"

"Already sent a rider to Pueblo with it. That's out of my jurisdiction. I'll have to let Sheriff Bowen take over. But I'll go see him tomorrow, see if I can help."

"Do you believe now that Muley Reece was one of the kidnappers?"

"Sure looks like it. I let him lead us into those canyons, and I think now he led us all around the mulberry bush."

"Has he ever been in trouble with the law before?"

"Not that I know of. I can believe he'd be in on it, though. He's been digging his heart out for too many years and couldn't find enough gold to even pay for his chuck."

"So he wouldn't turn down a chance at some easy money."

"Prob'ly wouldn't."

The day was shot. Now that the sheriff was gone, Pettigrew chopped some firewood, peeled and cut up some potatoes, carrots and what little beef he had and put it all in a pot. He waited until the fire had died down to hot coals and put the pot on to cook. At that altitude it took a good four hours to cook a stew. He wished it would rain and wash the blood off the weeds over by the creek. He wished it would rain and make the grass grow.

Just before sundown he found and corralled his horses, turned the roan loose and kept a bay gelding up. About an hour before the stew was done, he checked the fire and put more wood in the stove. The meat would probably be tough, but the only other meat he had was a slab of bacon. He would have to spend some of the few dollars he had left on groceries.

How the humped-up hell, he asked himself, did he ever get so broke? When he thought of it the answer was simple.

He'd quit the Pinkertons without an explanation, just a short note to the superintendent at Denver saying he no longer wanted to be a detective and to send any monies due him to Canon City care of general delivery.

With his wages and a reward from the JS Ranch in the Territory of New Mexico he had enough to buy out two homesteaders. They were happy to sell. There was too little rain for farming, and they couldn't get irrigation water to run uphill. The river and Cripple Creek were good for livestock, however, and Pettigrew used most of the rest of his money to buy seventy-five cows whose calves had just been weaned and ten old bulls.

The shack on the adjoining homestead was ready to fall down, so he moved into this one. He was ready to be a cowman.

He had a good calf crop, all right. Had to. He was riding all day and half the night, making sure those longhorn cows didn't die calving. He'd learned what it was like being a cowman, shoving his arm up a cow's rear end, straightening a calf so it would come out right. But so far he'd lost only one cow and a bull. What he didn't figure on was the time it took to realize a profit. Calves had to grow before they were ready for market. Most cowmen didn't drive beeves to market until they were two or three years old, and he didn't realize how much land it took to graze eighty-five head of cattle. One old cowman told him later that he'd better figure on at least fifty acres per cow. No wonder those cattle outfits in Texas and New Mexico Territory were so big.

One thing he did right was pick his spot. The tall timber country to the north was good grazing land in the summer, and down here on the river flats was a good place to winter cattle. Most of Colorado was open range, but, lordy, it took a lot of riding. He could use two or three more horses.

He could use more money.

While he ate his supper by lamplight he tried to figure out what to do next to earn that reward. First he had to figure out what the kidnappers would do next. He needed answers to too many questions. Did the kidnappers know that Muley Reece was killed before he could mail the ransom note? If so, would they change their plans? If not, would they be looking for old man

Atkinson to deliver the ransom? Would Atkinson do as they said? Would Sheriff Bowen of Pueblo stay out of it, as the kidnappers demanded?

Mulling it over, Pettigrew had no answers to those questions. He did believe, however, that the kidnappers would leave the canyon country. But go where?

Let's see. They wanted Atkinson to put the money in a white flour sack and tie it to a sage bush west of Pueblo and south of the river. There was a lot of flat country over there. A damned desert. With their glasses the kidnappers could see the white sack a long distance away. They'd watch Atkinson come and go, and they'd keep watching until they were sure no lawman was around. Where would they watch from?

The Sierra Mojadas to the south.

Sure. They'd be hidden in one of those *arroyos* that came out of the high hills. They'd stay put until the middle of the afternoon, then send one man to pick up the money. They'd turn the woman loose or kill her.

Meantime, they'd move camp. "Hell," Pettigrew swore out loud when he thought about it. They didn't give Atkinson much time to gather the cash. One day. Tomorrow. And deliver it next morning. They had to move closer. They'd probably moved today while Pettigrew was in town. They were camped tonight somewhere in the eastern foothills of the Sierra Mojadas.

Once they got the ransom they'd head over the Mojadas, cross the grassy valley on the west and get into the Sangres and then into the territory of New Mexico. From there they could go on south to Santa Fe or Albuquerque, maybe all the way to El Paso. They could cross the Rio Grande into Mexico and lay up with all the *putas* and tequila they wanted for as long as they wanted. Fifty thousand dollars would buy a lot of pesos. And with Muley Reece dead there'd be only two men to spend it.

Grinning, shaking his head, Pettigrew almost envied them. Were it not for the misery they were causing that woman, it would be a good plan.

Hell of a way to treat a woman, though. Pettigrew's grin vanished. Hell of a way to treat anybody.

Pettigrew's mind rambled on. The question was, would Atkinson do as they said? Yeah, he probably would.

Atkinson had refused to answer when Pettigrew had asked him about a ransom note. That meant he'd gotten a note before, and something went wrong. Yeah, that's what happened. The latest note warned him not to tell the sheriff anything, and said it was the second and last warning. Sure as shooting, old Atkinson had tipped off Sheriff Bowen in Pueblo the first time, and the kidnappers got wise.

Sheriff Bowen would know about this note, too. Sheriff Watson of Fremont County had read it and would tell him. Thanks to that dumb ass Muley Reece, the note was no secret. That meant the end of Mrs. Atkinson.

Unless Mr. Atkinson talked the sheriff into staying out of it this time. He could do that. He was the kind of man other men obeyed, even lawmen. If any lawman muddled things again and Mrs. Atkinson was killed, he'd be held personally responsible. What he ought to do, what Pettigrew would do if he were sheriff, was get up into those Sierra Mojadas and try to figure out where the kidnappers would cross, then waylay them. He'd have to do it alone, and he'd have to be damned careful. A posse would be too easy to spot. Yep, it would take a man alone to do it.

It would take Lem Pettigrew. And some luck.

Chapter Six

The horse he rode weighed around twelve-fifty, bigger than most. Big enough to carry some extra weight, like a bed tarp and blanket, and saddle bags filled with a coffee pot, a skillet, a slab of bacon, some boiled potatoes, coffee and a lard can half-filled with cooked beans. He had to carry the Winchester, too, in a boot under the right stirrup fender. Pettigrew could have taken a pack horse and more comforts, but two horses would have been easier to spot, and he wanted to travel light.

The horse he chose, a long-legged, long-backed bay, wasn't too handy at turning cows, but he was a good traveler and accustomed to being staked out on a thirty foot rope.

Pettigrew crossed the river below his cabin, then angled southwest at a high trot, wanting to get across the flats and into the foothills of the Mojadas as fast as he could.

This might be for nothing. One of the kidnappers might have drifted into Canon City late yesterday and heard about Muley Reece being shot. He'd think the ransom note hadn't been delivered, and they'd change their plan. Or they no doubt expected Muley Reece to meet them somewhere east of here today. When he didn't show, they'd get suspicious and change their plan.

Yet . . . maybe they wouldn't. They could believe that the letter hadn't been opened and was delivered by someone else to Charles B. Atkinson. By tonight they'd be sitting on the ground, casting mean glances at the woman, and trying to figure out what to do. If they went on with their plan, they'd be taking a gamble. The sheriff might be laying a trap, but their whole scheme was a gamble. As long as they had the woman alive they could use her as a shield. That was another reason this was a one-man job.

The foothills of the Mojadas were mostly weathered shale and sandstone, eroded into *arroyos* and draws. A few short junipers and cedars grew out of the high places. Cholla was everywhere. Cattle had grazed in the hills for enough years that they had made trails. Pettigrew had picked up a cattle trail that appeared to be headed into the higher hills and followed it to the top of a rocky bench. There, it disappeared. Reining up, looking up, he could see the tall timbers of the high country. That was where he wanted to go. He was taking a long, high route, but he wanted to stay out of sight and be where he could see what was happening in the foothills to the east.

"Well, Highpockets," he said to the long-legged bay, "we're gonna have to do some climbing."

From where he was he couldn't see a trail of any kind, so he picked a brushy draw and rode into it. For most of an hour the bay pushed through the buck brush, clambered over rocks and climbed. The brush picked at Pettigrew's clothes and boots, picked at his face and hands. His wide-brim hat provided some protection for his face, but his rein hand was soon covered with scratches. Where the draw shallowed out they broke out of the brush, and he looked down onto the flats. His cabin was only a small spot down there.

"Get your wind, feller," he said to the horse. "We've got a ways to go."

39

Climbing, always climbing. Most hills were too steep to climb straight up, and man and horse had to double back and forth, gaining altitude with each switchback. Here the rocks were changing to granite and deep valleys opened ahead. Across each valley was a higher ridge covered with tall pine and spruce and granite boulders as big as houses.

Reining up on top of a rocky pine-covered hill, Pettigrew looked down on a green valley and a small band of deer. "No use climbing higher," he said to the bay. "What we have to do now is work our way south and find a spot where we can see the end of the railroad and the river and the flatland south of the river. Stay high enough and we ought to see those jaspers without being seen. If they haven't been scared away."

Still angling southeast, Pettigrew and the bay stayed within sight of the divide, but under it, and when they broke out of the timber and boulders to where they could see below, he reined up and studied the terrain. The sun had reached its peak, but still he wasn't where he wanted to be. They kept going, uphill and downhill, through the timber and around boulders. Near an outcropping of white quartz, they went around a fifteen-foot-deep hole dug by a prospector who'd hoped to find gold or silver among the quartz. It had been a lot of work for nothing.

Another bunch of deer bounded across a grassy park ahead of them and disappeared into the woods. A redtailed hawk circled overhead, searching for a chipmunk or a gopher that was too far from its hole. At midafternoon they topped a rocky hill and were looking down at the river and the end of the railroad.

"Ought to see them," Pettigrew said. The bay was blowing hard from climbing. It cocked one ear back at its rider. The railroad was so far away that workmen looked like bugs, and the railcars looked like pebbles. But he could see the men clearly. If any of them left the railroad and crossed the river, Pettigrew could watch him. No other human was in sight.

"Well, like I said, Highpockets, this might be for nothing. If they expect to pick up a bundle of money early in the morning, they ought to be close to where they can see what's going on down there. They ought to be below us somewhere."

Man and horse moved on, dropped into a small bowl, skirted another prospector's hole, then climbed another hill. Again Pettigrew studied the scene below. "A lot of men at the railroad, but nowhere else," he said. Another dip and another hill later, and they were traveling through a stand of aspen with leaves shivering in the westerly breeze. The horse had to step over downed trees and around others that were too high to step over. Speaking to himself, Pettigrew allowed, "These trees grow fast and die fast. Where the quakies grow there's no shortage of firewood." Then they were out of the woods again. Down there was the remains of a small settlement. Hardscrabble, it was called. He'd heard about it. Somebody had built a store to sell goods to the prospectors and anybody else who came along. A few folks had built cabins and settled there, but business was too slow, and the entrepreneur had moved on. So had the rest of the population. Hardscrabble was a ghost town.

Or was it? A thin spiral of smoke came out of one of the clapboard shacks.

As soon as he saw the smoke, Pettigrew turned the horse back into the aspens, out of sight, and got down. He tied the bay to a tree, then walked back to the spot, bending low, trying to make himself hard to see. There was human life down there. Lying on his belly, Pettigrew strained his eyes. The high country sun beat down on his back. It had to be them. Two men and a woman. One horse was staked out near the shack. No—it wasn't a horse, it was a long-eared burro. Why would they have a burro? And where were their horses?

The way he'd heard it Hardscrabble was home only to packrats and maybe some skunks and porcupines. Yet the burro was tied on the end of a long rope, and somebody was cooking something in that shack.

"Well, whatta you know?" Pettigrew mused. He lay there, hoping to see a man come out of the cabin, then finally got up and went back to his horse. He led the horse out of the aspens to a grassy park, pulled the saddle off and picketed him on a thirty foot rope. "Eat and rest," he said. He took some cold biscuits and some strips of cooked bacon back to the spot. There he sat cross-legged, ate and kept his eyes trained on the scene below. Sooner or later they would show themselves. If they were smart they'd be keeping an eye open for lawmen. They'd take no chances. If they had a lookout, he was well hidden.

For over an hour Pettigrew watched. Still, the only sign of life was the burro, lying down now. Somedambody was in that shack, and whoever it was ought to come outside. Nodambody stayed in the house all day. Maybe it wasn't the kidnappers. Maybe it was a prospector — but he ought to come out.

Looking at the sky, Pettigrew figured it was about four hours until dark. If the kidnappers were down there and were dumb enough to stay inside, he might be able to Indian his way up to the shack and get the drop on them. If it wasn't the kidnappers, he'd sure like to know who it was. Whatever he did, he had to do it before dark.

Talking to the horse, he saddled up again. "Didn't get much rest, did you, feller? Well, it's downhill from here." He stayed in the timber and off the skyline as much as he could as he worked his way down to the foothills. Every time he came in sight of Hardscrabble, he stopped, dismounted and studied the scene carefully. Nothing changed, except that no more smoke was coming from the shack. Dinner was over down there, Pettigrew muttered. "Sombitches ought to come outside to pee, if nothing else."

In places, the horse slid on its haunches and in other places it climbed. But most of the route was downhill. When they came to a brushy gulch which appeared to end near the settlement, Pettigrew turned the horse into it. "Too bad you don't have a hard head and horns like a cow," he said. "Too bad I ain't built like a plowshare. Watch where you put your feet. Don't want to fall." Twice he had to stop the horse and part the green scrub oak with his hands before they could go on. After an hour and a half of that they came to the shallow end of the gulch. They weren't far from the shack now.

Pettigrew got down and tied the horse to a thin limb and hoped he wouldn't pull back and break loose. Carrying the Winchester, he made his way out of the brush and squatted on his heels just under the edge of the gulch. Carefully, he raised up enough to see the shack. Only the burro had changed. It was standing, looking his way. Still no sign of human life.

The store had been built of board and batten with a false front and a porch with a roof over it. The roof had caved in on one side, and the porch boards were rotted and broken. A handful of shacks stood silent and vacant, with doors and windows wide open, roofs sagging. Grass and weeds grew in what was once a street.

Only one shack, the one with a stovepipe sticking out of the roof, looked fit to live in.

Pettigrew estimated it was two hundred yards to the shack. Two hundred yards, with no cover. The door and one window was facing his way. The window had glass in it. A man or men could be standing inside watching him. Somebody was inside. Or somewhere near.

"All right, Lem Pettigrew," he muttered to himself. "What now?"

He'd be a perfect target running up to the door. What he ought to do, he decided, was circle and come up behind the cabin. He'd have to do it afoot, and stay out of sight. The country around two sides of the settlement was rough, rocky and full of gulleys. Getting behind the cabin wouldn't be easy, but he could do it. Yep, that's what he'd have to do.

Carrying the Winchester, Pettigrew went back into the buckbrush and worked his way to the side of the gulch. When he climbed out of the gulch, he was in view of the shack, and he quickly dropped to his hands and knees. He crawled. Hanging onto the rifle made it awkward. This for damned sure wasn't going to be easy. Now he was in a wide draw with a few scrub cedars. He hurried from one cedar to another until he was behind a shale outcropping. There he crawled to where he could see the shack.

Still no change. The burro was looking toward the bay horse. It couldn't see the horse from there, but it knew another equine was in those bushes. That was good. Any man who suspected anything would be looking in the direction the burro was looking.

Yeah, sure, Pettigrew thought. They could have had him spotted all along. They could be just waiting until he made a good target of himself.

Well, hell, either go on or go back.

Crawling on hands and knees, running bent low, he splashed across a narrow creek and worked his way to the other side of the settlement. Everything looked the same from that side. Where were their horses? The shack had no window in the back. Pettigrew was squatting in a grassy draw where only his head could be seen from the settlement. To get to the shack, he would have to cross fifty yards of open land. But at

44

least nobody could shoot him from a window. He figured he had two choices: he could run like hell to the shack and hug the wall, or he could walk carefully, eyes peeled, rifle ready to fire. Or maybe he'd be better off with the sixgun in his right hand. He could aim and fire it faster.

"All right, Lem Pettigrew," he muttered. "Let's see if you can keep from blinking."

He stood straight and walked, eyes straining to catch any movement, anything at all. He walked with swift steps, holding back an urge to run. When he reached the shack, he stood with his back to it. Nothing happened. Whoever was in there must have been asleep. Taking a late siesta. He sure as hell wasn't worried about anybody sneaking up on him.

Walking with slow, careful steps, Pettigrew moved around the shack, stopping several times to look and listen. He squatted under the window, then slowly raised up to look inside.

A man's voice came from behind him. "Don't move one inch, mister. Don't move a hair."

Chapter Seven

Pettigrew moved only his head as he tried to look back. He couldn't turn his head far enough, and started to twist his shoulders.

"Stand still. Stand right there. This forty caliber will make oatmeal out of your spine if you move any more than I tell you to."

Pettigrew stood still.

"Now, move very slowly, but do as I say. Let the hammer down on that handgun and drop it." When the Colt hit the ground at Pettigrew's feet, the voice said, "Now the rifle." The rifle hit the ground. "Now, without any sudden moves, turn around." Pettigrew turned.

The man facing him was slender, bareheaded and nearly bald, with a bushy brown beard. He wore baggy wool pants held up by elastic suspenders and he had lace-up boots on his feet. Somehow his soft brown eyes didn't look dangerous.

But that long-barreled breech-loading rifle in his hands was pointed right at Pettigrew's middle, and the hammer was back.

For a moment, neither man spoke, each eyeing the other. Then the man with the rifle said, "Tell me all about it."

"About what?"

"About why you're pussyfooting around here with guns in your hands."

"Pussyfooting? Oh, well, I'm looking for somebody."

"Do you want to kill him, whomever he is?"

"Not unless I have to."

"Tell me about him."

"There are two. Two men and a woman. The woman was kidnapped."

"Are you an officer of the law?"

"No. I'm a private citizen."

"You're after a reward." It was a statement, not a question.

"You know about them, then," Pettigrew tried to figure out where the man had come from. He saw nothing to hide behind.

"It was in the newspapers."

The rifle barrel hadn't wavered, but the man holding it didn't seem to be the dangerous sort. Pettigrew stood easy now, relieved. "You're a long way from town."

"I get to town once in a while."

"You live here by yourself?"

"As long as I've got this rifle aimed at you I'll ask the questions."

"Well." Pettigrew shifted his weight from one foot to the other. "I didn't come here for the fun of it. I think it's likely that the kidnappers are coming this way. In fact, they probably already have. I thought they might be in this cabin."

"They didn't come this way."

"I can see that—but I'll bet they came near here. They could be around here now."

"What makes you think that?"

"I've got a reason. Uh, listen, I'd feel better if you'd aim that long gun somewhere else."

The rifle didn't waver. "What's your name?"

47

"Pettigrew. Lemual Pettigrew. I've got a half-section just east of Canon City. I mean you no harm, whoever you are."

The rifle was lowered. "If you think some kidnappers are coming this way you'd better pick up those guns."

Pettigrew picked up the guns, holstered the Colt and held the Winchester pointed down. "I told you my name. Mind telling me yours?"

"I'm nameless."

With a shrug, Pettigrew said, "I reckon that's your business."

"Mr. Pettigrew, I learned some time ago that the way to keep out of trouble is to stay away from it."

"Can't argue with that. Listen, I've got a horse tied in those scrubs over there. I'd better go get him before he leaves the country."

The man with no name glanced at the sun, about to disappear behind the mountains on the west. "It will be dark soon. Do you want to continue your search tonight?"

"Maybe not. Maybe first thing in the morning."

"Bring your horse over here. I'll be in my house."

Pettigrew walked toward the scrub oak. The bay horse was so glad to see him that it nickered in a low gasp. "Come on, Highpockets. Let's be sociable." He led the horse back to the cabin. The man had gone inside.

"Hello," Pettigrew said to the cabin door. The door opened.

"You're welcome to stay the night if you care to. You can picket your animal near the creek."

Glancing at the darkening sky, Pettigrew allowed. "It's gonna be a black night. No moon. Those gunsels will either show up here in the next hour or so, or they won't show up 'til daylight. Or they're already down there somewhere."

"Whichever."

"If they show up, you'll need some help defending your cabin. If they don't, I won't find them in the dark anyhow."

Pettigrew offsaddled the horse, led him to the creek to drink, then tied him on the thirty-foot rope far enough away from the burro that the two wouldn't get their ropes tangled. Then he picked up his saddlebags and stepped through the cabin door.

It was one room, lined with tarpaper except for a sheet of plywood tacked to the wall behind the two-hole stove. The wood had been scorched by heat from the stove. An iron bed with springs was against the far wall, covered with a U.S. Army blanket. The table and two chairs were hand sawed from scrap lumber, no doubt scrounged from the remains of other cabins. A smoke-blackened coffee pot sat on the stove, and something was simmering in a covered iron pot. Firewood was stacked beside the stove.

But it was not the usual prospector's cabin. There were books. Homemade shelves stretched across two walls, and each shelf held books. Pettigrew guessed there were at least twenty-five volumes. From where he stood in the door he couldn't see the titles, but they were well-used. One lay open on the bed.

The man with no name saw Pettigrew eyeing the books, and said, "Do you like to read, Mr. Pettigrew?"

"Yeah. Yes. Those must be classics."

"They are. They are the only thing of value I own. Except for this Remington Creedmoor rifle. And it, you may have noticed, is not a weapon. With its peep sight, it is designed for paper shooting."

"Paper shooting?"

"Target shooting. I was the official county champion back in . . . never mind where."

49

"Well, I don't want to put you out, Mr. . . . uh, and it'd be better if I slept outside anyway. If those gents come along, we don't want to be trapped in here."

"Which means you don't care to stay for dinner. I wish you would. I don't have many visitors."

"Well, uh, yeah, all right."

"I can hang a blanket over the window, Zeke usually lets me know if any stranger, human or animal, is near. Zeke, you may have guessed, is my donkey."

Grinning, Pettigrew asked, "Did he let you know I was near?"

"He did. And getting behind you was easy." He pointed at a small crack between two wall boards where the tarpaper was torn. "I saw you coming, and when you went around the house that way, I slipped out the door and went around the other way."

Pettigrew chuckled. "Well, I'll be damned."

"Anyway, I led my donkey to Pueblo and back only a few days ago, and I've got some cured ham and fresh vegetables. Would that suit your palate?"

"Sounds good, but I've got some bacon in these saddlebags that's gonna spoil if we don't eat it. Save your chuck."

"Whichever."

It was black outside when they sat at the table, tin plates heaped with boiled potatoes and turnips and thick slices of bacon. They ate in silence, but when the meal was finished and the man with no name tamped a long-stemmed pipe with tobacco, Pettigrew leaned back in his chair and said:

"Mr. uh, nameless, you've probably met a hundred gents like me, but I've never met anyone like you. I apologize, but I'm breaking out with curiosity."

The man struck a match, got his pipe going. "My past is past. Buried and forgotten. Now I'm a nonentity." Two puffs of smoke came from a corner of his mouth. "I want nothing to do with society. I'm just an observer. A silent observer."

Pettigrew didn't know what to say to that, so he said nothing.

"Do you know, Mr. Pettigrew, who the wisest man on earth is?"

"Can't say I do."

"A tramp. A common tramp. He spends all he gets on himself. He owns nothing, but sees lots. He has no old age nor illness. He just dies. Do you understand?"

After thinking it over a moment, Pettigrew said, "I understand what you're saying." He stood. "I'll wash the dishes and then I'll unroll my blankets outside."

"I have only one bed, but no doubt you're accustomed to sleeping on a hard surface. You're welcome to a spot on the floor."

"Thanks, but I'd rather be outside in the dark in case somebody comes prowling around."

"Whichever."

As he lay on his bed tarp, a blanket over him, his boots under the blanket with him, Pettigrew tried to guess at what had turned the man with no name into a hermit. He was well-educated, but something had happened to him sometime, somewhere.

Oh well. Pettigrew turned onto his side. He's harmless.

At first light he was up, shivering in the cold morning air. He led his horse to the creek to drink, then saddled him, repacked his saddlebags and rolled up his blankets. He was chewing on some cold bacon left over from supper when the cabin door opened and the bearded bareheaded man appeared in it.

"Leaving already?"

"Yeah. The men I'm looking for either ain't coming or they've picked a spot farther downhill."

"I have some chicken eggs, and I prepare an excellent omelet. You're welcome to stay for breakfast."

"Thanks. I appreciate that, but I've got to be on my way." Pettigrew swung into the saddle.

The bearded man came outside where he shivered in the cool air. "I have a request."

"Sure."

"Please don't tell anyone about me. I knew when I found this spot that I couldn't stay hidden forever, but I'm enjoying the solitude while it lasts. I don't suppose you understand."

"I'll keep your secret."

"Thank you kindly. You can come back if you care to."

"Thanks for the supper." The bay horse moved out readily, and Pettigrew soon had the ghost town of Hardscrabble behind him. He mumbled to himself, "They say it takes all kinds to make a world. Well, I just met one more kind."

He was at the bottom of the mountains now, but still on high ground. When he rode up a long cedar-studded ridge he could see the plains below. It occurred to him that he ought to leave his horse somewhere and walk. A man on a horse was too easy to see, and if those gents were smart, they'd sure be watching in all directions.

If they were down there at all.

What he should have done, he decided, was leave the bay at Hardscrabble. It wouldn't hurt him to walk a few miles, and it was downhill, too. If he saw those yahoos he couldn't just ride up to them. Yeah, best to go back to Hardscrabble, picket the horse, then walk.

"Hallo-o," he yelled at the cabin. "It's Lem Pettigrew." When the nameless man opened the door, he said, "I didn't know how close to the flatland I was. Mind if I leave my horse here? I'll stake him out where he won't be in your way."

"When do you think you will return?"

"Soon. I think. Either I've made this trip for nothing, or something's gonna happen pretty soon."

"Very well. The coffee's ready."

"I've got no time to spare. Thanks anyway."

He offsaddled and picketed the horse. Carrying the Winchester, he began walking. The ground was rocky and uneven, and walking wasn't easy. "Maybe this ain't such a good idea either," he mumbled. He stayed in the draws and *arroyos* as much as he could, and when he had to climb to higher ground, he bent low, even crawled on his hands and knees at times. The sun popped up on the eastern horizon and struck him squarely in the face. Squinting, hat brim tilted low, he went on, mumbling to himself, "Walking back uphill is gonna be hard work. This is all for nothing. What kind of a damn fool am I, anyway?"

Next time he climbed out of an *arroyo,* he saw the railroad, way over there. And the river, with a few trees growing along its banks. He lay on his belly and studied the country. Men were moving at the railroad. Smoke came out of a railcar, and the antlike figures were all moving toward that car. It was breakfast time for the workmen. There were also four flatcars loaded with something—ties and rails, probably. A waycar was on the end of the line.

Nothing moved near it. No engine was in sight. On the other side of the line of railcars was a corral with six or eight horses in it. Though they were far away, Pettigrew could see they were big horses, harness horses.

"Huh," he grunted. "They might have enough

53

steam power to pull all those heavy cars, but they need horsepower to build a railroad."

Would Mr. Charles B. Atkinson show himself down there and do as he was told? So far he hadn't. No sign of any kidnappers either.

"Aw hell," Pettigrew muttered, "this is a damn fool idea."

If the kidnappers were anywhere around they were farther downhill in a dry *arroyo* or draw, behind a scrub oak or a cedar or something. Pettigrew was going to have to keep moving until he spotted them, or give up.

Staying on his hands and knees, hanging onto the rifle, he crawled until he was in another gulch, crawled out of it and then into another. Dammit, they were either around here somewhere, or nowhere. This was a good spot to watch from. Pettigrew climbed out, ducked behind a juniper, lay on his belly and scanned the country. "Aw hell," he muttered, "this is . . ."

Then he saw them.

Chapter Eight

It was their horses he spotted first. Three of them, saddled and ready to ride, hidden in a wide draw. Not more than four hundred yards downhill, the horses were loaded, with blanket rolls and saddlebags tied behind the cantles. Pettigrew's eyes soon picked out the men. One was on his belly, watching the railroad through field glasses. The other was sitting on a small sandstone ledge behind him, out of sight of the railroad.

They were doing exactly what Pettigrew had guessed they would do.

The one without glasses looked uphill, keeping watch. When his gaze swept past him, Pettigrew froze. Damned sun was shining right in his face. His face might be reflecting the sun like a piece of glass. But then the man was looking to the north. Pettigrew hadn't been seen.

Exhaling with relief, he wondered where the woman was. Was she already dead? Hell, if those yahoos expected Charles B. Atkinson to leave money for them, they didn't need the woman. Why drag her along? If they'd already killed her Pettigrew was too late. Too late to claim the reward, but maybe he could rescue fifty thousand dollars. If he could do that he ought to get a percentage of it. But damn, he wanted that woman to be alive.

She'd been alive not long ago when she'd written

the ransom note. That might have been the last thing she ever did. But maybe she was tough enough or tricky enough to survive. She was an Easterner, a lady of refinement. But she liked to ride horses and she liked to shoot guns at targets. That's what Pettigrew had been told by one of the possemen. That woman, the posseman had said, had even wanted to go elk hunting. Mr. Atkinson allowed her to ride astride a horse and shoot her expensive English-made rifle at cans and bottles, but hunting was for men only.

It was her riding that got her kidnapped. She had a fine-blooded mare that her husband had shipped from somewhere back East, and she had a stable hand saddle that mare at exactly seven o'clock every morning. The beautiful, red-haired Mrs. Atkinson would mount her horse and go for a gallop into the desert near Pueblo — Everybody knew about that. And when she returned, the mare sweating and blowing, she instructed the stable man to lead the mare in big circles until it was cool and quiet. While the stable man was doing that, Mrs. Atkinson had breakfast brought up to their hotel room.

When she didn't come back one morning, the sheriff and all the mounted men he could round up went looking for her. They located the mare, but not Mrs. Atkinson. What they did find were hoof prints left by three other horses. After an all-day search they reckoned the lady had been kidnapped. And when a ransom note was found under a waycar door, they were certain.

Charles B. Atkinson was almost out of his mind. He swore that if anything happened to his wife he'd never rest until the culprits were hanged or shot. If necessary he'd use all his resources to track them down. He promised a thousand dollars reward to anyone who would find her and bring her back alive. Next day he raised the offer to five thousand dollars.

Now two men down there were waiting for him to pay fifty thousand dollars, and pay it without even being sure his wife was still alive.

Would he do it? Pettigrew lay on his belly in the dirt and rocks and watched to see.

Yes.

A man had crossed the river and was riding south. A man alone. Carrying a white sack.

He was too far away to be recognized with the naked eye, but that yahoo with the glasses would probably recognize him. He had him spotted. He lowered the glasses, turned his head and spoke to someone, then put the glasses back to his eyes. The someone he'd spoken to came from behind an outcrop of sandstone and knelt beside the man with glasses. Pettigrew squinted into the morning sun, trying to get a better view.

That someone wore a long skirt, divided, riding boots and a man's hat. Long red hair hung from under the hat. It was a woman.

It was Mrs. Atkinson.

Way down there the man riding south paused and looked toward the mountains. After a while he rode on. Then he stopped again, as if trying to decide what to do. If it was Atkinson, he was probably wondering whether his wife was still being held hostage, or was dead. The kidnappers figured it the same way, and ordered Mrs. Atkinson to stand and make herself visible. She even waved.

That was why she was still alive. To show her husband he wasn't giving away fifty thousand dollars for nothing. Or at least to make him think so. Also, Pettigrew guessed, she would be a shield while the two gunsels were getting away.

Sure. They'd keep her alive until they crossed the

divide and were on their way down the other side of the Mojadas, then they'd probably kill her.

Everything was going the way the kidnappers had planned. Atkinson was delivering the ransom, and there wasn't a lawman in sight. Now Atkinson was on the ground, tying the sack to a sage bush. He stood still a moment, looking up at where he'd seen his wife, then he mounted his horse and rode at a lope back toward the river.

What now?

Now, Pettigrew guessed, they'd wait. Be patient and wait to be sure nobody else was around. Wait until midday, probably. Then one man would go get the money while the other kept watch and guarded Mrs. Atkinson. Pettigrew decided to wait, too. He might, if he was careful enough and lucky enough, be able to Indian his way down there and get the drop on the two, but it would be easier if there was only one. Yeah, wait until one went after the money, then move.

Crawling backward, he got out of sight of the pair, sat cross-legged and prepared for a long wait. One thing he'd learned as a Pinkerton agent was patience. Waiting was hard, but the man with the most patience usually won. That's something the Indians had learned. All good hunters had learned it too.

After a half-hour he crawled back to his spot under a juniper. They were still there. One was scanning the country with the glasses. He watched the railroad cars, then turned onto his back and scanned the mountains behind him. Pettigrew ducked and crawled backward out of sight.

If there was a lawman down there at the railroad he was hidden among the laborers. Atkinson might have been talked into allowing at least one of the sheriffs to come along as far as the end of the railroad. That one might be watching with field glasses too. If so, he wouldn't accomplish much. About all he could hope to do was get a look at the man who went after the money so he could recognize him if he ever saw him again.

Pettigrew's stomach reminded him he hadn't had enough breakfast. "Too damn bad," he said. If he could do what he hoped to do he'd be eating a good steak tonight in Pueblo's finest restaurant. Until then, his stomach would just have to growl.

Again, he crawled back to his juniper. Still there. The woman was sitting on the ground, leaning back against the sandstone. Nobody was pointing a gun at her, but she had no chance to run. No matter which way she ran she'd be a good target. And she couldn't hope to out-wrestle two men. They didn't have to tie her up, just make her understand that if she didn't do what they said she was dead. They were no doubt telling her now that in a few hours she'd be free. Waiting must be hard on her, too.

When the sun was straight overhead, Pettigrew took another look. Sure enough, one man was moving. He was coming back to the draw where they'd left their horses. As Pettigrew watched, he untied a horse from a short cedar, tightened the cinch and mounted. Pettigrew ducked as the man took another long look at the high country. Then Pettigrew heard the clatter of iron-shod hoofs on the rocks. The kidnappers were carrying out the next step of their plan.

It was time for him to carry out his.

He waited until the gunsel was down on the flats and riding at a cautious walk toward the money sack before he left his spot and began working his way downhill. The high ground was covered with loose sandstone and shale, and it was impossible to walk quietly there. His knees were sore from crawling, but it was the only way. From a cedar to a scrub

59

oak to a juniper. Hanging onto the rifle. Then he got into a dry wash where years of snowmelt had left a sandy bottom. That got him closer. But when he looked over the top of the wash he knew he wasn't close enough. No matter which way he approached, he was going to have to make a target of himself. And damned if he was going to be on his hands and knees when he did.

All right, Lem Pettigrew, he muttered under his breath, it has all come down to this. Unless that gent is deaf and blind, one of us is likely to get shot. Better not be me. Holding the Winchester in his left hand and the Colt sixgun in his right, hammer back, he stood.

The man wore a dirty grey hat, jackboots, denim miners' britches and a faded plaid shirt. He was on his knees and his back was to Pettigrew as he watched his partner below. The woman was also on her knees, also watching. They both heard Pettigrew at the same time. Both spun. The man grabbed a lever-action rifle, but he was too slow bringing it around. Pettigrew was holding the pistol straight out with the middle of the man's chest in the sights. He was too close to miss.

He said, "Stay right where you are and put the gun down."

A curse came out of the man. The woman gasped.

Pettigrew yelled, "Put it down. Do it now or you're dead."

The rifle dropped to the ground.

"Who . . . ?" the man sputtered. "What . . . ?" His mouth was opening and closing, but no more words were coming out. The woman was wide-eyed but silent.

"Get down," Pettigrew barked. "On your belly." When no one moved, he barked again. "Down.

Now. Or I'll shoot."

"God damn it, who in hell—?"

"Shut up! On your belly," he ordered.

Slowly, the man stretched out, face down. The woman was still staring at Pettigrew, eyes wide. Pettigrew walked over to the man, reached down and took a hogleg pistol from a holster on his right hip, then stepped back.

Now he could look around. There was no one else. He could see the mounted gent below, riding toward the white sack. Good. Pettigrew had been afraid a gunshot would send that one riding for cover. This was working exactly the way he'd hoped it would.

Backing up a few steps, he sat on a rock and smiled at the woman. "Mrs. Atkinson, I'd guess."

"Who—who are you?"

"My name's Lemual Pettigrew. I'm a rancher."

"What, uh, how did you . . . ?"

"You've been wondering what happened to Muley Reece? I shot him."

Understanding came into her eyes. Her chin came up. "You're the one . . . oh, I see."

"How are you, Mrs. Atkinson? Are you hurt?"

"No. I'm not injured. What are you going to do now?"

She was beautiful. In spite of straggly hair and a dirty face, in spite of a torn blouse and a smeared skirt, she had class. Something about the way she held her shoulders, the way she looked into his eyes, the way she now had herself under control.

"I'm gonna take you to your husband. But I don't want that hoodlum down there to get away. I think we'd better wait 'til he gets back."

The man on the ground started to rise. "Stay put," Pettigrew barked.

"Listen, mister." His black bearded face was

61

turned to Pettigrew. He was no one Pettigrew had ever seen before. "There's fifty thousand dollars down there. You're not a lawman. You can use a cut of that money."

"Sure," Pettigrew said.

"Well then, how about we give you half and you go back to your ranch?"

"And what would we do with Mrs. Atkinson?"

"Aw, shit."

"That's no way to talk in front of a lady."

"She's no lady, mister."

With a wry grin, Pettigrew asked, "What do you think of that, Mrs. Atkinson?"

A brief smile touched her face. "I like your plan better, Mr. Pettigrew."

"Then I reckon we wait."

She picked up the field glasses and aimed them downhill. "Look—he has the bag. He's coming back. We won't have to wait long."

Chapter Nine

Sure enough, the rider below was coming at a lope, carrying the white bag. Pettigrew handed the prone man's sixgun to Mrs. Atkinson. "I've heard that you can shoot."

She took the gun in both hands, handled it as if it were something nasty. "Yes, I can shoot a rifle, but I've never handled a pistol."

"You do it the same way. Cock the hammer back and point it at him. If he moves or yells, shoot him."

"What are you going to do, Mr. Pettigrew?"

"Get the drop on that other feller when he gets here, and take the money."

"Be careful of him. His name is Homer, and he's very dangerous."

Pettigrew yanked the prone man's hat off his head and put it on his own head. Then he carefully looked around the tree and watched the man named Homer come. Homer slowed to a trot and held up the white bag.

"We got 'er," he yelled. "We got 'er!"

Something behind Pettigrew moved. The gun in Mrs. Atkinson's hands roared. Wheeling, Pettigrew saw the other man running as hard as he could run. The woman's voice was high, near hysteria. "I missed. I'm not accustomed to handguns. I missed him." The sound of the gunshot was bouncing back from the hills. Then Pettigrew's head jerked to his left. Homer was spurring hard, riding north, carrying the white sack.

Pettigrew swore. He barked at the woman, "Wait here."

He took off running himself, boots clattering over the rocks. He had to get on one of the horses and get after the man with the money. Stumbling, skinning his knee, he jumped up and ran. He got to the draw just in time to see the first man stepping onto a horse. "Stop," he yelled. "Stop or I'll shoot."

A rifle cracked somewhere to the north. Pettigrew pulled up suddenly, wondering. The man on the horse reined up. Another gun popped, and the man pitched out of the saddle, hitting the ground heavily. He lay still. Hoofbeats were coming this way. Pettigrew stood his ground. Men on horseback appeared on top of the draw, reined up a moment, then came on.

Pettigrew glanced around for cover. The buck brush. That was his only chance. He started to run for it, stopped. The rider in the lead was wearing a silver star on his shirt. When they drew up, Pettigrew recognized the kid deputy from Canon City.

Pettigrew holstered the Colt, and said nothing as four men dismounted in front of him. One was carrying the white sack. Two thoughts went through Pettigrew's head: it was over now, and the woman was safe. But it was a posse who'd get the credit—and the reward. Then suddenly his heart jumped into his throat and his blood froze. He was looking into the big bore of a shotgun.

A cruel, ugly face was behind the gun. It said, "Well now, looks like we hit the jackpot."

For a few seconds, all Pettigrew could see was the hollow end of the scatter gun. One twitch of the man's trigger finger, and his head would be blown off his shoulders. He sputtered, "What the holy hell . . . ?"

Deputy Ellsworth sneered, "I figured it was you down here. Thought you'd be a hero, didn't you?"

Pettigrew's throat was tight as he spoke, "It's, uh, it's all right now. The woman is safe."

Still sneering, Deputy Ellsworth said, "Is that so? You're all set to collect a reward now, ain't you."

"Yeah. It's, uh, it's all over now."

"Haw." The outburst came from one of the others, a man with a flattened nose and a bill cap. "It's all over for *you*, mister."

The shotgun was still aimed at Pettigrew's head. "What . . . what do you mean?"

"You dumbshit cowpoke." The deputy's sneer had faded. "You was gonna settle for five thousand dollars. Shit, we're gonna settle for nothin' less than fifty thousand."

Now he understood. Fear was turning to cold anger. "Why, you son of a bitch."

"Why don't I just scatter his brains all over the county?" It was the ugly with the shotgun talking.

"Wait a minute. Sheriff Watson is down there somewhere. He'll head for where the first shots came from. We don't want to bring 'im over here. Not yet."

"Well then, how about this?" The one who spoke wore his pants legs inside high-topped boots. He reached down and pulled a long-bladed knife from a sheath inside the right boot. "This don't make no noise."

A wicked grin spread over the deputy's face. "Yeah. This dumbshit made a fool of me back in Canon City. You can cut his damned head off for all I care."

"Turn around, mister."

Pettigrew could only stare in horror.

"This is gonna be like bleedin' a steer. Turn around, mister, or I'll stick this Texas toothpick in your eyes, one at a time."

"No, by God." Again, the fear was turning to anger. "If you're gonna kill me you'll have to face me when you do it."

"Brave son of a bitch, ain't you?" The ugly advanced, holding the knife shoulder high. He waved it slowly in front of Pettigrew's face. Pettigrew couldn't keep his eyes from following it.

Then two things happened: The knife wielder stepped between Pettigrew and the shotgun and the woman hollered.

"Mr. Pettigrew," she yelled, "someone's coming. Two men are riding . . ." She had appeared on top of the draw they were in. When she saw the men, she stopped and stared, unbelieving.

"Get her," Deputy Ellsworth yelled. Two men started toward her, but she wheeled and ran out of sight. "Get her, God damn it," he screamed.

Pettigrew grabbed the knife hand, and at the same time butted the man in the face with his head. His hat softened the blow, but the man staggered back, tripped and fell. Pettigrew dropped with one knee on the ugly's crotch. He yanked his right arm across the other knee and bore down. The man yelped in pain, and the knife hit the ground.

"What the hell!?" Ugly with the shotgun had been watching the chase, but now he turned, holding the gun waist high. Pettigrew had no chance at grabbing the gun. He did the only thing he could do—he ran.

Heading for a clump of buck brush at the head of the draw, Pettigrew ran as fast as he could move his feet. The shotgun boomed. Pettigrew's left leg suddenly went numb, and he fell. Grimacing with desperation, he jumped up and hopped on one foot a few steps, then fell again. As he fell, a sixgun popped and a .44 slug slammed into the ground just beyond his head. Pettigrew rolled into the brush, hidden for the moment, but not for long. They'd come for him. Twisting, turning back on his belly, looking through the branches and leaves, he saw a man running toward him, carrying a pistol. Pettigrew drew his Colt and fired a quick shot. That stopped the running

66

man, but the other, the one with the shotgun, was re-loading.

"I'll get that son of a bitch."

"Why in hell didn't you take his God damn gun away from him?"

"I'll get 'im," was the grunted reply.

Feeling was returning to Pettigrew's left leg. He ignored it and tried to get the shotgun ugly in the sights of his Colt. He fired, then cursed himself for not taking better aim. As fast as he could he crawled backward into the brush.

Pain was like a tearing, searing knife in his left leg now. Teeth bared, he tried to ignore it as he waited for the thugs to come crashing into the brush after him. He'd get at least one of them.

But they didn't come into the brush after him. They didn't have to. They could climb out of the draw and look down for him. There wasn't enough scrub here to hide in for more than a few minutes.

The woman screamed. Screamed again. He knew they'd caught her and were dragging her back. He had to move, and move fast. No time to crawl.

Hanging onto a scrub oak limb, he pulled himself up. He was surprised to find his left leg would hold him. He took a tentative step, grimacing with pain. The leg worked. The woman was sobbing now.

Favoring his left leg, Pettigrew pushed his way through the scrubs, hoping that no one was waiting for him with a shotgun when he came out. Before he left the scrubs he dropped to his belly again, raised his head and scanned the country. The shotgunner was there, off to his left and a little uphill. Immediately, Pettigrew pulled back. A blast of buckshot hit the ground so close that dirt stung his face.

The gun was a single shot, a breach loader. It would take a half-minute to reload it. Pettigrew rose up again, hoping to get a shot at the gunner. No. The gunner was behind two junipers, out of sight.

The sound of boots on shale spun Pettigrew's head in the other direction. Another pugugly was up there, ready to shoot. Pettigrew snapped a shot which missed but drove that one back over the top of the draw. Then he cocked the hammer and waited for the shotgunner to show himself.

He would have to shoot fast and straight. He held his breath, waiting, afraid to blink.

A man yelled, "Hey, c'mere! C'mere! Hurry, God damn it."

The yelling distracted Pettigrew for a half-second, long enough for the shotgunner to step out from behind the junipers. But Pettigrew got off a shot before the gunner could take aim. Another blast of buckshot kicked dirt in his face.

Then there were footsteps running away.

For a few seconds, Pettigrew couldn't see. And when he wiped dirt out of his eyes with a shirt sleeve he was surprised to discover that not a man was in sight. For a moment he lay there, not convinced he was still alive. Finally, rolling onto his back, he looked down at his left leg. Blood had soaked through his duck pants just above the knee. Blood had run down his leg into his boot. The leg throbbed. Each throb felt like a hammer blow.

The leg had caught some buckshot pellets, that was for sure. Pettigrew didn't know how far he could travel on it. But he had to get away from there.

Chapter Ten

More yelling and a rifle shot came from behind him. Two more rifle shots. Pettigrew could guess what was happening.

The woman had said somebody was coming. Two men, she'd said. Probably one of the sheriffs and Mr. Atkinson, coming to look for her. They were shooting it out with four killers.

He considered going back to help the sheriff. If he could come up behind the uglies, his sixgun could make a big difference. But when he stood, a sharp pain knifed through his leg. He took a tentative step. The leg held him up, but walking hurt like hell. No matter how the gunfight ended back there, at least two of the killers would survive and come back this way.

Gritting his teeth, Pettigrew mumbled, "Walk, you fool. Get those feet moving."

He walked, climbed out of the draw, holding onto the Colt and dragging his left foot. If he could walk as far as his horse, he could ride, and if he could ride he'd make it to a town, Pueblo or Canon City. Hopping on one foot at times, dragging the other foot at times, he went on, heading for Hardscrabble.

The man with no name had heard the gunfire. He stayed in his shack, rifle ready, and watched through the window, wondering what had happened. A man appeared off to the east. The man was dragging one foot, falling, getting up, coming on a few steps, falling again. No-name recognized Pettigrew, and hurried out to help him, clutching his long-barreled rifle.

Pettigrew was standing again when No-name reached him. He tried a grin, but the grin turned to a grimace.

"Let me help you," No-name said. "You are obviously badly injured."

With a second weak grin, Pettigrew said, "It's only one leg. I've got another."

The man with no name got his right shoulder under Pettigrew's left armpit. "Put some of your weight on me."

"I don't want to cause you any trouble," Pettigrew said through clenched teeth. "There was some shooting back there. I don't know what happened, but it's trouble."

"Save your strength. Try to keep your weight off the injured leg."

"If you'll help me saddle my horse, I'll get out of your life. You don't want me around. My middle name is Danger."

"Don't be foolish." The bearded one was the support that Pettigrew needed to hop his way to the shack. Inside, No-name got Pettigrew seated on the narrow cot, and said, "Let's get your boot off and your trousers."

"Listen, mister, there are men over there who'd cut your throat for a dollar. They'll track me here, and they want me dead. They'll kill you too."

"I know nothing about that, and I don't care to know."

"You said just yesterday the way to keep out of trouble is to stay away from it. You'd better let trouble get away from you."

"I do know that you need help." He lifted Pettigrew's left foot. Ignoring protests, he pulled the boot off. "Now, unbutton your trousers and let's get them off."

"Uh, I don't want to get caught with my britches

down. Unless the sheriff back there is a hell of a gun-fighter, those killers will be here."

"Very well. I'll keep watch. But first let me look at your wound." He paused and let out a long sigh. "I am a doctor, you see."

"You're a what? You're joshing."

"No, Mr. Pettigrew, I am not joshing."

"Well, pardon my curiosity, but . . . ?"

"Perhaps one day I shall make myself known. Perhaps not."

"Huh? Well, anyhow, Doctor, I've got to lead those thugs away from you. Where'd you put my boot?"

"Stay where you are. I'll keep watch."

"You're in a lot of danger with me here."

"So be it. I'll keep watch." No-name went to the window. "Oh my. There are four men over there."

Pettigrew stood, clenched his teeth at the pain. "They ain't here to be sociable. We're in for a fight, Doctor."

"I wish no conflict with anyone. However, if they insist"

A "Hallo-o," came from outside. The doctor picked up his rifle, held it in his left hand as he opened the door a crack. "Yes?"

"I'm Deputy Ellsworth from Fremont County, and we're looking for a man name of Pettigrew."

Pettigrew cursed his own carelessness when he discovered that his Colt held only one live cartridge. Hastily, he punched out the empties and reloaded with .45 cartridges from his gunbelt.

"May I ask," the doctor said, "why you are searching for Mr. Pettigrew?"

"It's criminal business. Is he in there?"

The doctor looked back at Pettigrew. "He says he's a deputy sheriff."

"He is, but he's a crook and a killer. Don't trust him." Pettigrew hopped on one foot to the window. The four were there. And the woman, astride a horse, her hands bound to the saddle horn.

To the man with no name, he said, "That woman is

Mrs. Atkinson. I almost had her rescued."

"Then those men are hoodlums and scoundrels. I will not allow them in."

"Get that long gun ready."

Deputy Ellsworth was on the ground. "We're gonna have a look in your cabin."

The long-barreled rifle was held hip high. "Come no closer."

"You're interferin' with an officer of the law."

"I think not."

"We're comin' in anyway."

The rifle cracked. A puff of dirt jumped up in front of the deputy's feet. The crack of the rifle was deafening in the shack. Deputy Ellsworth swore, "God damn it. Scatter. Get the bastard."

"Get back away from the door, Doctor. Shut it." A bullet tore through the wooden door, leaving a splintery hole. "Dammit. Wish there was a window on the other side."

The doctor was calm. "There is a porthole. I have nailed some boards over it. Whoever built this house wanted to be able to defend it."

"Where?"

Without answering, the bearded doctor pulled the cot away from the wall and used the butt of his rifle to knock a board loose. He looked through a square hole, then immediately put the barrel of his rifle through it, aimed and fired. "That gentleman," he said calmly, "doesn't know it, but I could have shot any button off his shirt."

"You'd better let him know it." Pettigrew fired at a running man, but his short-barreled sixgun wasn't accurate at that distance. "They're out of sight on this side," Pettigrew said.

Another rifle slug tore through the door and knocked a book off a shelf. "Why," the doctor said, "that is *Candide,* by Voltaire, one of my favorites. The scoundrel will regret that."

The same rifleman fired a shot through the window,

missing Pettigrew by two inches. Pettigrew spotted the gunsmoke and fired back. His bullet went wide. "Dammit, wish I had my rifle. See anybody over there?"

"No. They have withdrawn."

"Bring that long gun over here, will you. I see that low life that wanted to cut me."

Hurrying to his side, the bearded one peered out. "Show him to me."

"Over there across the creek. Uh-oh, he's backed out. No, there he is. Lend me your rifle."

"I see him too." The doctor put the rifle to his shoulder, squinted through the peep sights and squeezed the trigger. Shock waves rolled through the shack. The doctor said, "I hit a granite boulder near his head, and he will feel the reverberations for some time. Now they know we mean business."

"You missed? You hit a rock near his head?" Pettigrew's tone was incredulous and accusing.

"I hit what I aimed at. At this time it is not my intention to kill anyone."

"Aw . . . well, will you let me borrow that gun?"

"If it becomes necessary to kill, I will kill." The doctor's tone was quiet and utterly certain.

"Well, it's gonna be necessary. Didn't you see that woman, the way she was tied to the saddle?"

"Yes. If I could rescue her by shooting all four of those hoodlums, I would not hesitate to do so."

"That's the only way to rescue her."

The doctor stepped back, his eyes engaging Pettigrew's. "Mr. Pettigrew, I spent six years in a university learning to save lives, not take them."

Shrugging, Pettigrew said, "Anyway, they might be pulling out. I don't see anybody out there." He crossed the room and looked through the square porthole. "Nobody out here either."

"They are leaving. I see them riding their horses up Hardscrabble Mountain. There are five."

"I guess they figured we're forted up too good here and we ain't worth getting shot for." Pettigrew sat on the cot to take the weight off his left leg. "They've got the woman. Her life ain't worth a plugged nickel now." His shoulders slumped, and he shook his head sadly.

The nameless one said, "Terrible. The poor woman. Perhaps I . . . perhaps I should have shot to kill."

Still shaking his head, Pettigrew said, "They'd kill her anyhow. If we'd shot two of them the others would have killed her and run for it."

"What do you think they will do?"

"What the kidnappers planned to do. Go over the Mojadas, get across the valley. They can go a lot of places from there. They'll keep her alive only long enough to see if anybody is following them."

Both men were silent a moment. Pettigrew stood. "I've got to go after them. It's another one-man job."

"You can't. You can barely stand. Your wound will fester and become infected. Then you will either lose your leg or die. Blood poisoning is fatal."

With a pained expression, Pettigrew pleaded. "You're a doctor — can't you do anything? I've got to get after them."

"I'll do what I can. Please sit down and take off your trousers."

Pettigrew hesitated a moment, then sighed and unbuttoned his pants. Sitting on the cot, he pulled off his right boot, then pulled his pants off. The bearded one opened a wooden box at the end of the room and removed a black satchel. He said, "These are the tools of my trade." He bent over the bloody leg. "You have multiple wounds here. Were you shot with a shotgun?"

"Yup," Pettigrew grunted.

"Very well. First I must heat some water and dissolve some carbolic powder. Then I shall wash the wound and use my needle forceps to pick out the particles."

"I'm lucky you're a doctor."

The man with no name soon had a fire going in the cook stove. He placed a pot of water over an open burner. "At this altitude, water boils at a low tempera-

74

ture, but it should be hot enough to sterilize my forceps."

"I guess," Pettigrew said slowly, "that you're not gonna tell me why you're living here alone."

"Some things are better left unsaid."

When the water was warm, but not hot, the doctor dipped a cloth in it and washed blood from the wounds. Pettigrew counted four small holes in his leg, just above the knee. "Will you lie on your stomach, please. I suspect there are more wounds."

He did as asked, lying on his belly in his shirttail and shorts.

"I was right. You were moving away from the man with the gun."

"I was running like hell."

"Uh-hmm." He pulled the table over next to the cot, lit a lamp. By then the water was boiling. Pettigrew turned his head and watched as the doctor put long, needle-nosed forceps in the water. In a minute, the doctor was back. "I regret to say I have neither morphia nor chloroform. If you feel like yelling, yell."

Searing hot pain shot through Pettigrew's leg as the doctor probed for the first pellet. Pettigrew clenched his teeth and kept quiet. A pellet was dropped into a tin pan on the table. Then the forceps went in for another.

It took only twenty minutes, but to Pettigrew it seemed to take forever. Would this never stop? Finally the doctor spoke. "Now, Mr. Pettigrew, will you please turn over onto your back."

"Umph," Pettigrew said. He rolled over.

The nameless man put the forceps back into the boiling water for the fourth time — or was it the tenth time — then returned, and the torture began again. Pettigrew held his right arm over his mouth to stifle a groan.

"I think we have them all now. Nine."

Relieved, Pettigrew said. "I didn't catch the full load, then. Good thing. It would have taken my leg off."

"What we must do now is wash the wound thoroughly with carbolic soap."

Trying to joke, Pettigrew said, "I need a bath anyhow."

The wounds were soon dressed in white muslin, and the patient pulled his pants back on. The left pant leg was crusted with blood. He stood. "Feels better already."

"It will be sore for some time. You appear to be a healthy young man, with the proper care you will heal. However, you must keep the wounds clean."

"I'll do it. Right now I've got to saddle that horse out there and ride."

"Oh no. You mustn't. Wait until morning."

"I'm much obliged to you, Doctor. I've got my wallet here, and I'll pay you." He took a cowhide wallet from a shirt pocket.

"No. I am no longer a practicing physician. Had this not been an emergency, I would not have touched your wounds."

"You earned whatever you'll take."

"Nothing. I'll take nothing."

"You sure?"

"Yes." His expression permitted no further discussion.

Limping to the door, buckling his gunbelt, Pettigrew said, "Damn, it's getting dark. Well, I know which direction tbey went. I won't be far behind them."

"I wish you'd wait until morning."

"I wish I could." He pulled his hat on. "But I've got to ride."

Chapter Eleven

The long-legged bay horse stood patiently while he climbed stiffly into the saddle. Trying to hold his left knee away from the leather, he urged the horse forward.

"God damn," he groaned. "This won't do at all." Jaws clenched, he let the horse take a few more steps, then reined up. "Uhh. Can't do 'er. Hurts like hell." He got down, nearly fell when his left foot hit the ground, then limped and led the horse back to the shack. The bearded one was watching. "Just can't ride, Doctor. I don't guess there's anything more you can do."

Shaking his head, the man with no name said, "I have no anesthetic at all. A night's rest will help, but your wounds will still be sore in the morning. You're welcome to stay the night."

"Dammit, I keep thinking about that woman. She's going through hell, and I can't help her. Can't walk, can't ride, can't do anything."

"Don't you think that some officers of the law will come along looking for her?"

"Yeah, but no telling when. And when they come they'll come in a bunch, and those uglies have got the woman for a shield. Like I said, going after them is a one-man job."

"I know nothing of what happened today. When you left here the second time you were going to try to rescue the woman, Mrs. Atkinson. When you returned you were wounded and four dangerous-appearing men were soon behind you. The woman was obviously a captive."

Pettigrew told him about rescuing the woman and the ransom only to lose both to four killers. "The woman saved my bacon when she hollered that two riders were coming. They took after her, and that gave me a chance to run. I'm guessing they were Sheriff Watson from Canon City and Mr. Atkinson. There was a gunfight. The killers had surprise on their side, and there were four of them. The two men are either dead or wounded."

"I'm very sorry about everything, especially for the woman. But there's nothing you can do tonight. Besides, it's turning dark. Bring your bedding in here."

With a grimace, Pettigrew studied the ground at his feet, then said, "Well, I hope this leg is better in the morning." He picketed the horse again and carried his saddlebags and blanket roll inside.

Pettigrew smelled of the bacon he had left and the can of beans, and declared them fit to eat, but the doctor advised him to save his food. "If you're going over the mountains, you'll need sustenance, and I can go back to Pueblo for supplies whenever I need them." So they ate fried potatoes and carrots with a thin slice of ham apiece. That was topped off with thick slices of bakery bread and apple butter. "Not like dining at the Ritz," the doctor said, wiping his beard with a white handkerchief, ". . . but it is nutritious."

"It'll stick to your ribs," Pettigrew allowed.

After the dishes were washed, and the doctor was smoking his long-stemmed pipe, Pettigrew again tried to probe the doctor's past. "It, uh, takes a smart man to get through medical school. I couldn't do it. You must have done a lot of studying."

"Considerable, yes."

"Seems a shame to waste it. Lots of towns in the west need a doctor."

"It is illegal to practice without a license. Except in

emergency situations." The pipe smoke smelled good to Pettigrew.

Trying to keep a conversation going, he said, "I bought a pipe once and tried to smoke it, but it kept going out. You seem to like it."

"Done in moderation, smoking is harmless, and yes, I do like good tobacco." The man with no name was leaning back in his chair with his legs straight in front of him, puffing on the pipe.

"Moderation. That's the way to do everything, I guess." Pettigrew was beginning to feel foolish trying to draw something out of this man. Maybe he ought to shut up.

"That's a good word of advice." Two more puffs of smoke came from a corner of the doctor's mouth.

All right, Pettigrew thought. I'll try one more time and then I'll keep quiet. "A doctor is a valuable citizen in any town. Doctors are sometimes the most respected citizens there are."

That got a reaction. "Citizen? Hah." The bearded one stood, stomped across the room and sat again. "The best thing a man can do is nothing. Don't be a citizen at all. Just be an observer and remain silent."

Now that he'd got the man talking, Pettigrew remained silent.

"And by all means keep out of trouble. How, you may ask?" Now the doctor stood again and paced the floor. "If there's a meeting, stay at home. If there's a crowd, get out of it. Avoid women. Be celibate, a eunuch, if necessary. The male urges are terrible. The sins of the flesh are destructive, devastating. They have destroyed many a man."

Suddenly, the bearded one dropped onto his cot. He sat with his head in his hands a moment, then looked up at Pettigrew. "I do not wish to continue this conversation, Mr. Pettigrew."

Pettigrew had to clear his throat, "Well, ahem, it's time for me to hit the blankets. I'll sleep outside."

"No, uh, please excuse my outburst. In your condition you should sleep on the bed. I'll sleep on the floor."

"Naw. The floor ain't gonna hurt my leg, and I can't take your bed."

"Whichever."

The throbbing pain in his left leg kept Pettigrew awake for a while as he lay in his blankets on the floor. What I ought to do, he thought, is stay here a day or two until I can ride, then go home. At home I can heal. Tracking the killers is the sheriff's job, not mine.

On the other hand, the two kidnappers might have let her go if I hadn't showed up. She looked to be in pretty good shape. They couldn't have been too hard on her. Maybe they would have let her go when they got the money. It's my fault she's a hostage again, and my conscience has been damaged enough.

Conscience. He felt like snorting out loud. The happiest people were people who had no conscience. They could steal, rob, murder, and enjoy what they got out of it. A conscience could ruin everything. His conscience was what had prompted him to quit the Pinkertons.

That, and John "Beans" Gipson. Beans would be released from prison soon, and he'd be looking for Lem Pettigrew.

Pettigrew realized his thoughts were wandering, and he muttered, "Hell. One damned thing at a time."

He figured out a way to sit on a horse without unbearable pain. What he did was roll up his denim jacket and put it under his left knee. That held his injured leg away from the saddle. Awkward, but tolerable.

The doctor had washed and rebound the wounds. "This is definitely better than it was last night," he had murmured. "But you should stay off it for a week at least."

He could stand it as long as the horse moved no faster than a walk. Going away from Hardscrabble was all uphill and into the timber anyway, where it was hard for a horse to travel faster than a walk. The killers' tracks were easy to follow, but the color of the horse droppings told Pettigrew they had traveled at least part of the night. Within an hour the sun was shining between the tree tops, casting long shadows, winking at him as the tree tops swayed in the breeze. At noon, Pettigrew was still miles from the divide. An hour later he came to their first camp-site.

Dismounting, he walked stiffly, sorely, looking for some sign that the woman was still alive. Empty tin cans littered the site, which told him the four gunsels had planned this trip. They had brought enough chuck to last a while.

He ate cold beans out of the lard can and a piece of bread, and while he ate he guessed at what had happened. Sheriff Watson wouldn't have showed that ransom note to just anybody, but he did allow the kid deputy to see it. Deputy Ellsworth got together with some of Canon City's toughs and cooked up a scheme. It was the same scheme Pettigrew'd had, only, as the deputy had said, they didn't want a mere five thousand dollars reward, they wanted the fifty thousand dollars ransom. And the deputy, knowing he would be recognized, didn't plan on leaving any witnesses. Had it not been for the woman's yelling at the right time and the nameless doctor's long gun, they would have succeeded. Hell, they had probably succeeded anyway.

Pettigrew chewed fast and swallowed fast, then tightened the cinches and mounted. He tried to find exactly the best spot for the rolled up jacket, but no matter where he placed it, his sore leg touched the saddle now and then. When it did he couldn't help wincing. He was riding in tall timber, but looking ahead, he saw the sky, and hoped that that was the divide. But when he topped a ridge, he was disappointed to see another narrow valley below him, and another high timbered hill beyond that.

Pettigrew rode back off the ridge, out of sight of anybody who might be watching the trail. He dismounted and crawled on his hands and sore knees to where he could look across the valley. The valley was bare of trees. A few willow bushes grew along the bottom where sometimes there was snow runoff. Granite boulders seemed to grow out of the slopes. The grass was high, waving in a cool breeze. Six deer, three of them bucks with wide racks of antlers, grazed peacefully. Good grazing land.

For five minutes, Pettigrew studied the boulders and the slope beyond the valley. Finally, hopeful that nobody was over there watching the killers' backtrail, he mounted and started the painful ride downhill.

He'd learned, especially when he'd been horse packing, that a horse's back has more motion going downhill. That was when a pack was most likely to turn, and that was when his sore leg kept bumping the saddle. Gritting his teeth, he pushed on the saddle horn and stood in his stirrups, trying to relieve the pressure. "Oh, damn," he groaned.

At the bottom, he found a trickle of a stream where he let the bay horse drink. He stayed in the saddle, readjusted the rolled-up jacket, and again studied the slope beyond. Those wagon-sized boulders would make a good hiding place for a bushwhacker. So would the timber at the top of the slope. Pettigrew felt like a man with a target pinned to his shirt. With fear in his throat he rode on, cautiously scanning the area.

There was never any doubt that he was behind them. Five horses left sign a blind man could follow. While he rode, he tried to figure out what he would do when— and if—he caught up with them. No ideas came to mind. He would have to wait and see what happened.

More worrisome was the fact that he wasn't catching up. Their sign told him he hadn't gained a foot. Well hell, how can I, he asked himself. They can travel just as fast as I can. Faster. They don't have to worry about a possible ambush ahead. What in hell can I expect to do? He shook his head sadly. Just hope to get lucky, and keep going.

The sun had gone down behind the high hills to the

west when he looked for a place to camp. Sunlight filtering through thin clouds threw a pale red glow over the whole country. He couldn't follow tracks in the dark, and the bay horse needed a rest. He needed a rest.

At the bottom of another timbered hill, he found a small grassy park surrounded by tall trees and jumbles of huge granite boulders. The grass was high, and the park was just big enough to picket the horse in. As in most mountain valleys there was a small stream where rain water and snow runoff lazied their way downhill. He offsaddled and picketed the horse, but carried his blankets back under the trees. If anybody came looking, he wanted to be hard to find.

But he had to have a fire, smoke or no smoke. He needed coffee, and the bacon he had wouldn't keep another day. Either eat it now or throw it away, and he couldn't eat it raw. Dead tree limbs were plentiful where there were pine trees, and he broke up a limb to build a small fire. While the bacon sizzled, coffee water boiled and the can of beans warmed, he stayed back out of the firelight as much as possible. His left leg throbbed. He considered pulling his pants down and taking a look at it in the firelight, but realized that that would do no good. There was nothing he could do for it.

Meal ready, he stomped out the fire with his right foot, and ate in the dark. Between mouthfuls, he listened. The only sounds were his horse cropping the grass and the sigh of the breeze in the tree tops. The sky was full of stars. If he could have blanked the woman out of his mind, and if his left leg were well, he would have enjoyed all this.

As it was, he ate, rolled up in his blankets, and finally slept.

Pettigrew had heard of folks who were so poor they had to eat beans for breakfast. Well, he wasn't that broke, but the bacon didn't smell right and he threw it back into the woods for a coyote or a fox or whatever came along. He sure didn't need the back yard trots to go with a sore leg. At least he had coffee with his beans and bread. Shivering, he could have used his jacket to keep warm in the high country, but he needed it more for padding.

Horseback, he rode uphill, around boulders and through the trees. There were no trails, but the gunsels knew where they were going, and the tracks led Pettigrew over the easiest route. At the top of the hill, he could see for many miles in all directions, and he believed he was on top of the divide now. "It'll be easier going from here on, Highpockets," he said to his winded horse.

Sure. Easier on the horse, but harder on a sore leg. Wincing with almost every step, Pettigrew urged the horse down a steep hill, following a series of switchbacks. Then they were out of the timber and traveling a game trail, which kept to the side of a bare hill. Below were thick willows and a grove of aspens, above were more timber and boulders. But here the only vegetation was tall grass and a few low cinquefoil bushes. Trying to ignore the pain, Pettigrew kept his eyes busy, searching everything ahead. He reined up. At first he thought what he was looking at was a rockchuck or a chipmunk sitting on top of a low, round boulder about three hundred yards away. Those rodents liked to sun themselves. And even when it moved, he wasn't sure. But, squinting, eyes straining, he thought he made out a face under it. Was it a man's hat, or was he seeing men where there weren't any? Suddenly he hauled hard on the reins and turned the horse around.

Just in time to avoid the lead slug that burned the air over his head.

Chapter Twelve

Lemual Pettigrew cursed himself for not being suspicious sooner, for not knowing the difference between a rockchuck and a man's hat with a pair of eyes under it. But cursing did no good. He had to get up into the timber. Kicking the horse with spurless bootheels, whipping it with the ends of the bridle reins, he got it turned uphill. The slope was so steep the horse had to scramble, scratch for footholds and hump its back.

"I apologize, feller," Pettigrew said, "but if we don't get out of sight of that yahoo we're both dead."

Another rifle slug screamed off a rock near the horse's feet. The sound of the shot rolled across the valley. The horse scrambled, humped, grunted and dug for footholds. Then they were in the timber, safe.

Pettigrew allowed the horse to stop and blow. "Hell of a climb, huh, wasn't it, now," he soothed the horse.

He guessed the rifleman had a .44-.40, probably the most popular gun in the West. One reason was the short bullets that could be used in either a pistol or a rifle. But it didn't have the range that most of the sport rifles had. That gunsel knew it and had aimed high to allow for distance. He'd aimed too high with the first shot and too low with the second. If he'd had Pettigrew's rifle and some of the .45-.75 bottle-necked bullets, Pettigrew or his horse would be dead. Where was that gun, anyway? Then he remembered. It was way back there, where he'd rescued the woman. Or tried to was more like it, he thought.

85

All right, he said to himself, the shots had missed and he was safe, for now. But what had he accomplished? They knew he was behind them, and they'd be watching. Next time he got too close they wouldn't miss. He wouldn't even hear the shot. He'd just be knocked out of the saddle and dead before he hit the ground. What could he do?

Slumped in his saddle, he tried to think. What was ahead? Well, he'd heard about a wide valley between the Mojadas and the Sangre de Cristos. The Wet Mountain Valley, it was called. There was at least one town over there. Were the killers headed for that town? Where there was a town, there might be a stage line. If so, they could take a stage east to the Atchison, Topeka and Santa Fe railroad and travel by rail from there to Trinidad near the New Mexico border. From Trinidad they could go farther east to some city somewhere. If what Pettigrew had heard was correct, the railroad had built two routes to Trinidad. One came down from Pueblo and the other came southwest from somewhere in eastern Colorado. Yeah, they could be planning to do that.

But they wouldn't take the woman. They'd have to kill her. A hollow formed in Pettigrew's chest.

For a long moment, he sat his saddle, trying to figure out a plan. It seemed hopeless. Finally, he decided he'd have to risk it and keep after them. For now, he'd stay in the timber where the traveling was rough. Maybe they wouldn't be looking for him there. He urged the horse on.

It was midday when he could look down from a forest of pine and see where the bushwhacker had been. After a careful study of the country, he turned his horse downhill. Yep, there were two empty .44-.40 cartridge cases and bootprints. The shooter was a cigarette smoker, and had left a hand-rolled butt behind. He'd been waiting long enough to smoke one cigarette. Either he wasn't a heavy smoker or he hadn't waited very long. Maybe they weren't as far ahead as Pettigrew had feared. The tracks from there went through more timber — not a good place

86

for an ambush — and Pettigrew urged the horse into a slow gallop.

Riding downhill was rough on a sore leg. Riding at a lope was rougher. But Pettigrew had a terrible urge to hurry. It couldn't be far to the bottom of the Mojadas and to a town. The woman didn't have long to live.

He stopped when he came to a grassy park. He stayed under the trees and scanned the country ahead. A trail led across the park and into the woods on the other side. This trail was made by horses carrying men — better than a game trail. Maybe it led down out of the mountains. But Pettigrew had to go around all clearings. No more making a target of himself.

It took most of an hour to circle the park, but when he got back on the trail on the other side he saw no sign of a bushwhacker. Riding warily, he urged the horse into a lope again, gritting his teeth against the pain. The trail was clear, loaded with horse tracks and easy to follow. He let the bridle reins hang slack while he hung onto the saddle horn, trying to ease the pressure on his sore leg. The horse knew by now that it was supposed to follow the trail and needed no guiding.

Then they came to another small clearing at the bottom of a rocky hill, and again he stopped. Immediately, his eyes picked out the piece of cloth tied to a stick. The stick was stuck in the ground in the middle of the clearing. It had to be a trap. He was expected to be curious enough to ride out there in the open and take a look at it. Glancing at the sky, he saw the sun shining through high clouds close to the western horizon. He dismounted, favoring his left leg.

"Rest, partner," he said to the horse as he loosened the cinches. "We're not going out there in the daylight."

The killers were right about one thing: his curiosity about a piece of cloth on a stick had to be gratified, and if it didn't give them a chance to kill him, it at least gave them a chance to get farther ahead. He waited, stomach knotted with worry. While he waited he tried to eat. The bread had green spots on it, but he pinched them off and ate the rest. It tasted like sawdust. The cold beans were even harder to chew and swallow, but they were better than nothing. Dusk came. A half-hour later it was dark enough that he believed he could ride out there without being shot. He tightened the cinches and mounted.

At first he rode slowly, carefully, but then decided that was useless. He got the horse into a gallop again. At the stick he dismounted and picked up a piece of wrapping paper that was held down by a rock. In the near darkness he couldn't read the penciled message. Striking a match was taking a chance, but he had to do it. He lay on his stomach to make himself as small a target as possible, struck a match and read:

Sheriff Watson, or whomever you are, stay away. They will kill me if you come any closer. They have promised that they will let me go when they are safely away. Please do as they say. If they see any of you again, they will kill me.

It was signed Cynthia Atkinson.

They were using her as Pettigrew had known they would. But what was surprising was they hadn't recognized him. They thought he was the sheriff of Fremont County, and they thought he might have a small posse with him. Lem Pettigrew was wounded, they knew that, and should have been far behind, letting his wound heal.

Lying on his belly, Pettigrew tried to decide whether this was good news or bad. It was neither. If they thought a posse was after them they'd travel as fast as they could, but hell, they'd do that anyway. They hoped the note would slow a posse, but they wouldn't count on it. Nothing was changed.

By now it was dark, and he couldn't make out what kind of cloth they'd tied to the stick. It had to be a piece of clothing, and he doubted the killers had any extra clothes with them. That meant it was a piece of the woman's clothes.

"Oh, Lord," Pettigrew muttered as he mounted. "I hate to do this to you, Highpockets, but we can't rest.

Your eyes are better than mine in the dark. Just stay on the trail, will you?" He rode at a lope across the clearing, then slowed to a trot in the woods. The night was black, and he kept his right arm in front of his face, hoping to locate the tree limbs by feel before they hit him and dragged him off his horse. The bay horse wasn't tired yet. He trotted right along, keeping on the trail.

They went downhill a ways, then up a gentle slope. When they broke out of the woods, the quarter moon was high, and it put out enough light that Pettigrew could see a line of willows ahead. Willow bushes grabbed at his clothes as the horse pushed through. They splashed across a creek and crossed a stretch of boggy ground near the creek. He could hear the mud sucking at the horse's hooves, and feel the horse's back dip, hump and buck until they were on solid ground again. Jaws clamped, Pettigrew hung on.

"Just stay on the trail," he pleaded. Hell, he wasn't sure there even was a trail here. Mountain trails had a way of petering out. But he believed the horse was carrying him in the right direction. "Keep going, partner," he said.

The night wore on. The horse traveled on. But now the horse was tiring and had slowed to a shuffling trot.

When the horse stopped, he kicked it in the sides, and muttered, "Go on. Can't quit now. Keep going, feller." Then he reined up. "Something ahead? Do you see something, partner? What do you see? Wish you could talk to me."

He rode forward slowly, stopping every ten seconds to listen. They were in some woods where it was so dark he couldn't even see the horse's head. He listened. Then he heard it.

It was a horse blowing through its nostrils. A thump on the ground sounded like a horse taking a step. Yeah, there was a horse somewhere near. Listening, he decided there was more than one horse. He dismounted, and working by feel, wrapped the reins once around a low pine branch. He whispered, "If I don't get back you can pull loose and go somewhere. But don't pull loose for a while."

There was nothing but blackness ahead, but he guessed the men had camped in a clearing. Only in a clearing was there grass and room for their horses. Favoring his left leg, he crept forward, straining his eyes. He was sure he hadn't been heard. A man on guard might have heard his horse, but there were five other horses near, and he wouldn't know the sound of one from another.

Damn, it was dark. Pettigrew walked carefully, stopping to listen. He imagined the night was not quite so dark ahead. Creeping on, he realized it wasn't his imagination. He was near the edge of the woods, next to a treeless spot where the pale moon was putting out a very dim light. That was where they had to be.

For a moment he stood still, trying to decide what to do. He wished he were wearing Indian moccasins instead of boots. But even with moccasins it would take some luck to be able to creep into their camp and free the woman without making a sound. Yet that was the only way he could free her. Could he do it barefoot? He'd hate like hell to be caught in a fight in his socks. On the other hand, with his left leg as sore as a boil he couldn't run anyhow. He sat on the ground and pulled off his boots.

It was slow going. Slow and damned careful. Bending low, trying not to wince when he stepped on a rock, he moved into the clearing. Now he saw them. Just lumps on the ground in the dim moonlight. Two. There had to be more. Yeah, there were two more. All lying down, covered with blankets. There had to be another, a guard. One was snoring. Another farted. Which was the woman? He tiptoed closer. Where was the guard? And their horses?

Standing perfectly still, listening, he decided the horses were tied to the trees across the clearing. Not a good way to treat horses, but these uglies probably figured they were close to town and wouldn't need the horses much longer.

He saw the guard. He was lying on his side, knees drawn up, a long-barrel gun beside him. Asleep. Creeping closer still, he picked out the woman. She was the one lying close to another lump. So close they looked to be holding hands like lovers. It had to be her. Pettigrew couldn't remember seeing long hair on any of the men. Moving without sound, Pettigrew got even closer. Yeah, it was her. Now to wake her without waking anybody else. Holding his breath, he bent over her.

Dammit.

She was handcuffed to that son of a bitch next to her. Handcuffed. God damn. Now what?

Pettigrew backed off a few steps to think. That damned deputy had brought his handcuffs. Pettigrew couldn't cut handcuffs. It would be impossible to sneak the woman out of the camp. The more he worried about it the more he realized that there was only one thing he could do now. Could he do it?

Tiptoeing forward again, he looked for the deputy's pistol. Well, at least something was going right. The deputy had feared going to sleep with his gun within reach of the woman, so he'd left it on the ground out of her reach.

Trying not to breathe, Pettigrew took three steps, bent to pick up the gun, and backed away. The deputy stirred, and mumbled something. Somebody else stirred. Pettigrew froze. More mumblings. Breathing in shallow breaths, Pettigrew stood, almost invisible in the dark. Finally he dared take a step backward. His left leg almost collapsed when he stepped on a rock, but he gritted his teeth and took another step. Suddenly, he dropped to a squat. The man on guard sat up, gripping a gun, the shotgun. He had sensed something, or thought he had. But he wasn't sure or he'd have got up or hollered or both. Instead, he remained sitting for a long moment, then let his chin drop onto his chest.

Pettigrew let his breath out slowly, stood and backed away. When he was in the woods, he located his boots by feel, sat on the ground, pulled them on and waited for more light. He guessed he was fifty feet from the deputy.

Close enough for a pistol shot. But the shot had to be right on target.

If they knew he was alone, they'd fight, and there were four of them. But if they thought a posse was in the woods, they'd throw up their hands. Maybe. Maybe not.

When daylight came, Pettigrew would have to shoot fast and straight.

Chapter Thirteen

Pale light was slowly spreading over the clearing when the first man stirred. The party was about to begin. Pettigrew squinted down the barrel of his Colt .45 to see if there was light enough to shoot. Not quite.

Slowly, he stood and got behind a tree. In his left hand he carried the deputy's gun, probably a .44-.40. The caliber didn't matter as long as it would make a noise.

The guard awakened with a snort, and sat up straighter. It was still too dark to see his face. He stood, stretched and yawned. He would have to be the second target. The deputy was the next to sit up, yanking the woman's right hand up with him. She cried out in pain. The time had come.

Pettigrew kneeled behind the tree, aimed his Colt, got the deputy's chest in the sights and squeezed the trigger. Without waiting to see whether he'd hit his target, he fired the other gun. The two explosions in the quiet morning sounded like the world had blown apart. Men yelled. Men jumped up.

Pettigrew's next shot knocked down the man who was already standing. He fired again with the left hand gun without aiming, then took aim at another man with his own Colt.

"Jayses Christ!"

"It's the God damn law!"

Two shots were fired in Pettigrew's direction, but they

didn't come close. He kept firing the left hand gun until it clicked on empty.

"C'mon, Ellsworth," a man yelled. "There's a God damn army over there." Ellsworth didn't move.

"Where's the God damn money?"

Two more shots came Pettigrew's way.

"That bastard Ellsworth's got it. Sumbitch sleeps on it."

A figure moved toward the downed deputy. A bullet from Pettigrew's Colt changed his mind. "Dammit it," he swore.

Two men ran out of the clearing and into the trees. Two lumps stayed still. The woman was sitting up.

Pettigrew fired two more shots at the running men, then reloaded his Colt as fast as he could move his fingers. He heard horses snorting and shuffling their feet. Hoofbeats.

Then it was quiet. The only sound was a low sobbing coming from the woman.

Pettigrew waited a moment. Cautiously, he walked to the woman, knelt beside her. He whispered, "It's Lem Pettigrew. Are you hurt?"

"N-no," she stammered.

"Where's the key to those handcuffs?"

"In — in his pants pocket. The right one, I think."

"Get it while I keep watch."

Deputy Ellsworth suddenly inhaled deeply and tried to sit up. Then with a long sigh, he fell back and stayed still.

The woman asked, "Is he d-dead?"

"He'd better be. Get that key."

As if in a daze, she fumbled in the dead man's pockets and finally found the key. Pettigrew thought she would never get the shackles unlocked. When she stood, he said, "Come on — this way. Run."

"My boots."

"All right, pull your boots on, but hurry. Those gents might get wise and come back. We're in the open here."

Hopping on one foot at a time, she got the boots on. Pettigrew said, "Run. This way."

Run? She could, but he couldn't. Limping on a sore leg, he followed her out of the park and into the woods. "My horse is right over here. Get on him. Hurry."

The bay horse snorted when the woman hurried to him, but didn't try to pull away. Pettigrew helped her climb into the saddle. "He's going to have to carry double," he said. "Take your left foot out of the stirrup." She did, and he managed, by grunting and straining, to get on the horse behind her.

"Their horses were over there somewhere." He pointed across the clearing. "I hope they didn't take them all." Then he remembered something. "The money. Did the deputy have it?"

"Yes. He didn't let it out of his sight."

"We have to get it."

She turned the horse back to the campsite, where Pettigrew slid backward off the animal's rump. He turned the dead deputy over. The saddlebags were under his head. Cursing his fumbling fingers Pettigrew opened one of the bags, saw money and buckled the flap again. "Their horses can't be far away. I'll try to walk that far. If any shooting starts, turn that horse around and head that way, downhill."

Three of the horses were still there, tied to trees, still carrying saddles. One had broken its bridle reins, but had stayed with the other two. Pettigrew picked out a dun wearing an A-fork saddle and hung onto its reins while he pulled the saddles and bridles off the others. Mounted now on a strange horse, he said, "Let's go."

He hadn't known how close they were to the foothills of the Mojadas until they topped a barren ridge and looked across a wide valley. The sun, coming up behind them, was casting its light on the high peaks of the Sangre de Cristos across the valley. The Christos rose sharply into towering jagged peaks. Sunlight had turned the peaks into various hues of blue and purple. The valley was still in the shade.

With a weary voice, the woman said, "There's a town down there."

"Yeah. I see it. Wonder if they've got a sheriff."

They'd been riding quietly. Pettigrew wondered how the woman had been treated, but he didn't want to embarrass her by asking for details. He could tell that she was too worn out to feel like talking. He also wanted to know whether she'd seen the gunfight way back there on the other side of the Mojadas—whether anyone was killed, whether her husband was shot.

Finally, he had to ask, "You yelled that two men were coming from the railroad back there. Were they shot?"

With a long sigh, she said, "I saw them fall from their horses. I think one of them was my husband." A sob came from her throat. "I don't know whether he's dead or alive."

Hanging onto the saddle with both hands, he led the way down into the *arroyos* and gulches of the foothills. They were out of the tall timber now, but the trail took them around a few pines and a scattering of cedars. Approaching the town, they saw a wagon road ahead, but before they got to it a stagecoach pulled by four horses went past at a high trot, heading east. The sun was on top of the Mojadas now, spreading its light across the valley.

Silently, Pettigrew surmised that the four killers had planned to be in that coach. That was why they'd camped in the hills. They'd planned to get to the stage station just in time to get aboard, before any lawman heard about them and got suspicious. If things had gone their way, they'd be traveling east now with fresh horses pulling the coach and fresh relay teams ahead. A posse from Pueblo or Canon City couldn't have caught them on jaded horses. Pettigrew wished he and the woman were on that stage.

The two of them attracted curious stares as they rode down the main street. It was lined with a hardware store, a general store, two saloons, a cafe and a two-story wood frame hotel. Houses, built of a mixture of logs, wood planks and stone, were scattered in all directions from there, even in the gulches of the foothills. They stopped in front of the hotel. Three men, a woman and two kids came up and stared.

"Where'd you come from, mister?" a man in miner's clothes asked.

"Pueblo," Pettigrew answered. "We came over the mountains. Is there a sheriff here?"

"There's a deputy. Somethin' happen?"

"Yeah." Pettigrew helped Mrs. Atkinson down. She almost collapsed in his arms.

The woman in the crowd asked, "Is she hurt? Is she sick?"

"No. Just worn out. She's had a hard time."

The woman stepped closer. "Can I be of some help, ma'am?"

Mrs. Atkinson tried to smile. "I look terrible, don't I?" Her red hair hung to her shoulders, stringy, knotted. Her divided skirt was torn and her shirtwaist was dirty. Her face was smudged. "I, uh, can I get a room in the hotel?"

"Why, I believe you can, ma'am. If your husband will help you inside, my boy here will watch your horses."

"He's . . . not my husband. He—he came to my rescue."

"To your rescue?"

"Yes. It's a long story, and I'm very weary."

Pettigrew handed her the saddlebags full of money. "Take this, Mrs. Atkinson."

"Mrs. Atkinson? Ain't I heerd your name before?"

"She's had a . . ."

Before Pettigrew could finish what he'd started to say, the woman interrupted. "Ain't you . . . you wouldn't be the woman that was kidnapped? The one I read about in the Pueblo newspapers?"

"Yes. I am Mrs. Charles Atkinson."

"Oh, well then, let me help you inside."

Another man came up, and another boy. After Mrs.

Atkinson had gone into the hotel, leaning on the woman, Pettigrew asked. "Is there a place where I can put up these horses?"

A boy about fifteen answered. "Over at Sammy's. He runs the stage and he's got some extra pens. I'll show you." When he saw the way Pettigrew limped and the dried blood on his pants leg, his blue eyes widened. "You been shot, ain't you?"

"Naw. Just hurt myself is all. Soon's I get these horses watered and fed I'll take care of it."

It was only two town blocks to the yards of Sammy's Stage and Freight Co. A stagecoach was parked near a two-story board-and-batten barn, and a series of pole corrals held fifteen or twenty horses. Sammy wasn't there but a hostler stopped raking manure long enough to show Pettigrew which pen to put his horses in. Pettigrew watched while the hostler forked hay to them, then limped back to the hotel, carrying his saddlebags. The boy stayed at his side, brushed a cowlick out of his eyes to look up at him.

"How'd you hurt yourself, mister?"

"Well, to tell the truth, son, I was shot, but it ain't serious. I've got something to tell the deputy and I don't feel like walking all over town looking for him. Go and tell him I need to see him, will you? I'll be in the hotel."

"Yeah, yeah, sure. How'd you get shot?"

Pettigrew stopped and looked down at the boy. "I'll tell you, son, if you'll go get the deputy. Will you do that?"

Nodding excitedly, the boy said, "Yeah, yeah."

"I was in a gun fight. There are two dead men up there." Pettigrew nodded toward the Mojadas. "Two others that ought to be dead got away and they might show up here. Got it?"

"Yeah, yeah, sure."

"Now go get the deputy, will you?"

The hotel lobby had a wooden floor that creaked when Pettigrew hobbled across to a registration desk. A man with a handlebar moustache and black hair parted in the middle stood on the other side of the desk and watched

98

him sign his name in the registration book. He seemed to be good at reading upside down. "Lemual Pettigrew, huh? Canon City, huh? You the gentleman that rode up with Mrs. Cynthia Atkinson?"

"Yup. Which room is she in?"

"One-oh-two, but she don't want to be bothered. I just filled the bathtub in the ladies' room for 'er, and she's takin' a bath."

"Well, when you see her tell her which room I'm in and to come and see me or send somebody for me whenever she feels like it. And the sheriff or a deputy or somebody ought to be looking for me too."

Grey eyes grew suspicious. "You in trouble with the law?"

"Naw, but I've got something to report to the law."

"About that kidnapping?"

"Yeah, that's what it's about."

Inside the room, Pettigrew was pleased to find a tin pitcher of water and a tin wash pan. He sat on the narrow bed, took off his gunbelt, boots and pants and unwrapped the strips of muslin from his left leg. The wrapping was bloody, and he tossed it into a woven wire trash basket under a plain wooden table. Digging into his saddlebags, he found a piece of carbolic soap that the man with no name had given him, and he washed his wounds. His leg was sore to the touch, and the wounds were red, but there was no pus.

"Well," he grunted, "they don't look infected. Now what am I gonna wrap around them?" In answer to a knock on the door, he said, "Come in it's not locked."

Were it not for the nickel star pinned to his shirt pocket and the big pistol in a sagging holster, the man who entered wouldn't have looked anything like a lawman. He was short, husky, and wore a miner's cap and baggy denim pants held up with elastic suspenders. His face was so wrinkled and seamed, Pettigrew wondered how he managed to shave it.

His narrow eyes went over Pettigrew's bare legs and the red wounds, then he asked, "Your name's Pettigrew?" Without waiting for an answer, he asked another question. "That woman you rode in with signed her name Cynthia Atkinson. Somebody said she's the woman that was kidnapped up at Pueblo. Is she?"

"She's the one."

The lawman was incredulous, "No." He dropped onto the one chair in the room and stared open-mouthed at Pettigrew.

"She is Mrs. Charles B. Atkinson."

"Well, well. Is she hurt or anything?"

"I don't think so. But she's had an awful hard time."

"Well . . . well, what . . . ?"

"Listen, deputy, she needs rest, and she's got to get back to Pueblo as fast as she can. Her husband was in a gunfight trying to save her and she doesn't even know if he's dead or alive."

"Well, Sammy runs a stage to the railroad ever' mornin', but the stage just left. There ain't no other way 'less she wants to ride a buckboard. But even if she did she'd miss the train up to Pueblo."

"I can't talk for her, but I'm guessing she's too beat down to travel today."

"I won't bother her then 'til she's had a rest. But you've got some talkin' to do."

"I figured I did. Make yourself comfortable. It's a long story."

Chapter Fourteen

It was after noon when Pettigrew finished talking and answering questions. The deputy, who gave his name as Joseph Mulhay, took no notes, and that worried Pettigrew. "Am I going to have to do all this talking again to the sheriff or somebody?"

"Prob'ly will. The sheriff won't be back 'til day after tomorrow, but I prob'ly oughtta hold a inquest. I can do that right after I get them dead bodies down out of the hills."

"Can you find them? I'd as soon not get on a horse for a while. This leg needs a little time to heal."

"Yeah. I know that country. I've hunted elk up there. I'll get some help and some extra horses and go see if we can find 'em. Hope you ain't plannin' on leavin' town for a couple days."

"I was hoping to leave on the stage in the morning, yeah."

"Can't allow 'er. We got laws, and when somebody kills somebody, even in self-defense, we gotta know all about it."

"I understand that, but I've got a ranch to run and I can't stay here more than a couple of days."

Deputy Mulhay stood, hitched up his sagging gunbelt. "You'll stay 'til I say you can go. If that woman's story don't jibe with yours I might have to lock you up 'til I get this all sorted out."

Pettigrew grumbled, "Sure, sure."

101

The word had spread. When Pettigrew limped into the Rosita Mercantile, pants leg bloody, needing a shave, he drew stares from everyone in sight. But the store owner wasted no time asking questions until after he'd measured a yard of muslin and found a pair of the new Levi's pants, size thirty-three by thirty-three. Pettigrew would have to turn up the cuffs. There were four other customers in the store, but no one spoke. They only stared.

Then, "You're the one that rode in with that woman, ain't you? Is she really the one that was kidnapped up at Pueblo?"

"Yeah," Pettigrew answered, wearily. "Got any crackers or anything? Maybe some sardines?"

"What happened?"

"There was some shooting. She's all right now."

"Who got shot?"

"Some hardcases. Listen, I don't remember when I ate last or slept last. Got anything to eat?"

Back in the hotel room, he rewrapped his wounds, made a meal of sardines and crackers and flopped down on the narrow bed.

Lem Pettigrew slept like a dead man himself, lying on the bed wearing only his shirt, shorts and socks. His dreams were deep and vague and kept shifting scenes. There was the doctor with no name at Hardscrabble, Charles B. Atkinson, his old boss Sheriff Popejoy at Johnson County in West Texas, his childhood in the small town of Johnsonville, his work for the Pinkerton National Detective Agency, and John "Beans" Gipson. And there the dream dwelled for a time. It was a disturbing dream.

He'd been a deputy sheriff for four years, and resigned when his boss completed his term and didn't run for re-election. It was Sheriff Popejoy who suggested he work for the Pinkertons, and it was the glowing recommendation from the sheriff that got him the job. That, and the fact that he'd done enough work on the cow outfits in West Texas that he could hold down a job as a cowboy. Plus the fact that the JS Ranch in south Texas was losing cattle and needed some undercover detective work done.

Plus, the Pinkertons had no agent who looked at all like a cowboy.

It was an easy assignment. Once Lem Pettigrew got acquainted with a good-looking young cowboy nicknamed Beans it didn't take long to figure out what was happening.

Beans and an older man named Newt Waltham were stealing a few cattle at a time and hazing them into a corral hidden in the mesquites that grew along the Rio Grande. A crew of *vaqueros* drove the cattle from there across the river, delivering them to a Mexican rancher who had two hundred thousand acres to hide them in. The *ranchero* paid Beans and Newt about half the market price.

Pettigrew got suspicious when Beans ran out of dollars in town one day and couldn't talk a bartender into taking pesos. "God damn Mex money won't buy a piece of ass this side of the border," he'd complained. He shut up like a trap when Pettigrew asked where he got the pesos. Then Newt suffered a broken leg when a horse turned over on him, and Beans needed a new partner. Pettigrew had let it be known that he wouldn't mind raking in more than cowboy wages if he could do it without killing anyone. Beans had found his new partner.

One theft of twenty-five cows was all it took to gather enough evidence. But Pettigrew's work wasn't done. The worst part was yet to come. He had to testify in court.

In his dreams Pettigrew often saw Beans' face when he said, "I never believed you'd rat on me, Lem. I thought we was friends. I never believed you'd —"

It was a knocking on the door that woke him.

"Huh," Pettigrew snorted, jerking upright on the bed. For a long moment he couldn't remember where he was. The knocking persisted. Finally, "Yeah? Who's there?"

A muffled voice came through the door, "The proprietor, Mr. Pettigrew. I've got a message."

"All right, all right. Give me a minute." Bedsprings squeaked when he got up. He pulled on his new pants and went to the door in his sock feet. The clerk with the handlebar moustache stood there.

He said, "Mrs. Atkinson asked me to tell you that she would like to meet you downstairs."

"All right, thanks."

He washed his face in cold water, ran his fingers through his brown hair, and wished he had a comb. He knew his face bristled with several days' growth of whiskers, but he had no razor with him. His boots thumped on the stair steps.

She looked some better, sitting in the lobby, although she needed clean clothes. She even managed a small smile. Two young faces were pressed against the window pane from outside, looking in at her. The proprietor went to the open door and hollered, "Now you kids get away from here."

"I hope you got some rest, Mrs. Atkinson," Pettigrew said as he sat in one of four wooden chairs in the lobby.

"Yes. I had a bath and a nap. I was wondering, Mr. Pettigrew, whether you've talked to the officers of the law here."

"A deputy sheriff. He ought to be gone after the dead bodies now."

"Good. I'm sure he will want a statement of some kind from me too. I'm so weary I hope we can get this over with so I can get back to Pueblo."

"I told him you have to get back as fast as possible. He said a stage leaves every morning going east. I might have to stay a day or two."

"Oh, I hope not. I need your company."

"I hope not too, but . . ." He shrugged. "I've been an officer of the law myself, and I know certain matters have to be settled."

"Do you suppose we could have dinner together? I feel so . . . so embarrassed all alone."

"Sure. You bet. I'll buy a razor and try to make myself fit to be seen with a lady."

Seated at a table for four in the Home Cafe next door, they had roast beef, mashed potatoes and brown gravy.

She ate only half of what was on her plate. Pettigrew cleaned his plate and ordered a slab of pie made of dried apples. They ate silently. She seemed to be deep in thought, and he didn't want to intrude.

They went to their separate rooms after dinner. Pettigrew took a "whore's bath" out of the wash pan, and wished he'd had enough money to buy some clean shorts and socks. With only a few dollars in his wallet, he'd have to sell his bay horse to get stage and train fare, but once he got back to Pueblo, he'd collect his reward and be rich. Well, working-man rich.

"Uh-oh," he said aloud when the thought hit him. What if Charles B. Atkinson was dead? Would he get the reward he'd earned? Surely, the widow would see that he did. Everybody in Southern Colorado knew a reward had been promised. He sat on the bed thinking. Yeah, sure. Of course I'll get the reward.

Deputy Mulhay got back after dark. Pettigrew lit a coal oil lamp, pulled on his pants and again went to the door in his sock feet. His big toe on the right foot had worn a hole in the sock, but, oh well, the deputy had seen holes in socks before.

"We got 'em down and layed 'em out." Deputy Mulhay said, "and I just talked to Mrs. Atkinson and got her story. It checks exactly with what you said."

"Uh-huh." Pettigrew sat on the bed and motioned the deputy to the one chair.

"What I need now," the deputy said, shifting his gunbelt and sitting, "is to get a jury together. Say, oh . . . four or five good men that can read and write, however many I can find, and tell 'em all about it. You'll have to be there, but I told Mrs. Atkinson she could leave on the stage in the mornin'."

"I know she appreciates that."

"Yeah, poor woman. She's had hell. I sure ain't gonna give 'er no more trouble."

"But I guess I'll have to stick around tomorrow."

"Yup. Can't be helped. What Mrs. Atkinson tells me is you saved her life more'n once."

Shrugging, Pettigrew said, "I wasn't trying to be a hero. There's a reward."

"Yup. I heered about that reward. What Mrs. Atkinson tells me is you surely earned it."

"When can you hold this inquest?"

"Not 'til mornin'. Wish we had a telegraph here. The sheriff's gone down to New Mexico Territory to eyeball a horse thief they arrested down there, and I wish I could telegraph 'im to get back up here. But we ain't and I cain't, so I'll do the best I know how."

Pettigrew almost told about having been a deputy sheriff himself, but he decided he didn't want to get into a conversation about that. Instead, he said, "Know where I can sell a good horse? I don't care to ride back over those mountains."

"Sammy buys and sells horses, mules, jackasses, wagons and just about ever'thing else. How much he pays depends on how hard up you are."

Pettigrew managed a small grin. "I'll try to put on a good act."

He saw the stage off with Mrs. Atkinson and three other passengers in it. The woman carried the saddlebags full of money. It occurred to Pettigrew to ask for an advance against the reward, but he didn't want to admit that he was broke. Sammy turned out to be a short, wide man with a nearly new brown hat and baggy wool pants. Pettigrew asked for forty dollars for the bay gelding, but settled for thirty-five. That gave him plenty of money to get to Pueblo, where he would collect his reward.

The town of Rosita had no coroner, but Deputy Mulhay called the gathering of five citizens a coroner's jury anyway. The hearing, in the combination sheriff's office and one-cell jail should have been short, but each juror had questions, mainly to satisfy their private curiosities. They didn't even leave the room to reach a verdict:

The two unnamed men met their deaths at the hands of one Lemual Pettigrew of Fremont County, state of Colorado. Mr. Pettigrew shot them in the defense of a kidnap victim, one Mrs. Cynthia Atkinson of Pueblo County. Therefore, it is the verdict of this coroner's jury that Mr. Pettigrew violated no laws of the state of Colorado.

"You understand, Mr. Pettigrew," a well-dressed juror said, "that this was not a trial, and if at some time the sheriff or the prosecutor decides to file charges against you it would not constitute double jeopardy."

"I understand."

"You're free to go on about your business."

Pettigrew bought a new shirt to go with the new pants. The new Levi's denim pants were cut full to allow for shrinkage, and they were baggy and stiff. He wished he'd bought another kind. He had a good breakfast under his belt, and a beer would have tasted good. But he didn't want to have to answer questions about the woman and her kidnappers, so he stayed out of the saloons. Now was the time to follow the advice of the doctor with no name and give his sore leg a rest.

He was dozing lightly in his room when a knock on the door brought him to his feet. "Who's there?"

A barely audible voice came through the door, "The sheriff."

It wasn't the right answer. Pettigrew drew the Colt .45, and when he opened the door he didn't stand in front of it. Instead, he stepped back, partially behind it.

The man who rushed in had a sixgun in his hand too, and he wasn't Deputy Mulhay.

Chapter Fifteen

In an instant, Pettigrew recognized the man. He fired as the man was turning toward him, then immediately dove for the floor, rolled onto his back and fired at the second man in the doorway. Two guns boomed at once. A lead slug dug a furrow in the wooden floor near Pettigrew's right shoulder. The slug from Pettigrew's .45 slammed into the wall across the hall. Pettigrew thumbed the hammer back and was ready to shoot again, but by the time he got to his feet, boots were thumping down the stairs.

The first man flopped onto his back and tried to sit up, but didn't make it. Blood was spreading across the front of his shirt. He wore his pants legs inside his boottops, and he carried a long-bladed knife in a sheath inside his right boot.

Downstairs, someone yelled, "Hey! Hey, what's goin' on up there?!"

Pettigrew stepped into the hall. "Get the deputy!" he yelled back.

It wasn't hard to explain who they were or what they were after, but it was a little hard to believe they were that bold — or desperate.

"They thought I had the saddlebags full of ransom money," Pettigrew said to the crowd that had gathered. "They didn't know Mrs. Atkinson took them with her. If they'd known that, the stage would have been robbed."

"Mister, you're lucky you c'd shoot faster'n him," a miner observed.

"I've had some practice lately." Pettigrew dropped onto the chair and added, "Lord, I hope I don't have to shoot anybody else."

"You sure he's one of 'em? And the one that ran, too?"

"Yeah. See the knife in that man's boot? Just a few days ago he came mighty close to cutting my throat with that knife."

"They woulda kilt yu. Prob'ly with that toad sticker so as not to make any noise."

"They was sure as hell desperate desperadoes."

Pettigrew said, "I guess they are — were. They went to a lot of trouble to steal that money, and they had to give it another try."

The well-dressed coroner's juror said, "Well, Joe, whatta you think? Do we need another inquest?"

A worry frown wrinkled the deputy's face. "I dunno — we got three dead men, all killed by this man here. God damn, I wish the sheriff was back."

"Whatta you think he'd do?"

Looking at Pettigrew, face still wrinkled, Deputy Mulhay said, "I reckon I'm gonna have to lock you up. We can't have all this killin' here without an investigation."

The hotel proprietor was frowning, wringing his hands. He said, "Who's gonna clean up all this blood?" No one from the crowd answered him.

The one-cell jail had a wooden bunk. No mattress, no blanket. Pettigrew used his hat for a pillow. His saddle, saddlebags and blanket roll lay on the floor near the one desk in the sheriff's office. When the deputy brought him a sandwich and a cup of coffee for a noon meal, he asked for his blankets.

"All right, but I gotta search 'em first." Deputy Mulhay unrolled the blankets, shook them out and handed them through the bars.

Comfortable now, Pettigrew mumbled, "Well hell, I need a rest anyhow." He settled in for a little peace and quiet.

Sheriff Whitehall got back late the next day. Average height, a little paunchy, grey moustache. Grey flat-brim hat with a high round crown. Weariness was written on his seamed, weatherbeaten face. He listened to what his deputy had to say, took a long look at Pettigrew without speaking a word, then opened the outer door to leave. "I'm goin' home to get some supper. I'll want to know more about all this after I eat."

When the deputy brought Pettigrew his supper, Pettigrew asked him how the sheriff was taking the news of all the killings.

"Not too good. Ain't had this much happen since he got elected. Folks around here are pretty peaceful."

Pettigrew snorted, "Ain't had this much happen to me since I was born."

It wasn't until noon the next day that Sheriff Whitehall spoke to him. Standing in front of the cell door, the sheriff pushed his hat back, and studied Pettigrew silently a moment. "Where would you go if I was to turn you loose?" he said.

Pettigrew stood up, slowly. He looked the sheriff in the eye. "First to Pueblo, then home," he answered.

"Way I heard it you've got a ranch somewhere near Canon City."

"Yep. A little outfit, but it's mine."

"Wal, the district attorney's office is at Pueblo, so I have to keep you here either 'til I hear from him or I make a decision myself."

Pettigrew's eyes locked onto the sheriff's eyes. "So what's your decision?"

"That woman, Mrs. Atkinson, gave my deputy a good description of the four hoodlums that kidnapped her the second time. You gave him a description too. Them three dead men match the descriptions."

"I'm no lawyer, but that sounds like a pretty good defense," Pettigrew observed drily.

"Still, some folks think maybe them two was somebody you knew and had a fallin' out with."

"I guess some folks could believe that."

"Them two knew where you was stayin' and which room you was in."

"I've seen only one hotel in town, so it wasn't hard for them to figure out where I was staying. They knew my name. The hotel proprietor no doubt told them which room I was in." Pettigrew's patience was growing thinner by the minute but he struggled to keep his face from showing it.

Sheriff Whitehall studied the floor a moment, then said, "Wal, you're restin' easy, and the county's feedin' you. I'm still askin' questions. If I don't find no more evidence and if nothin' else happens, I'll let you go in the mornin'. The eastbound leaves for Pueblo then, and I reckon you can be on it."

"I appreciate that."

"Meantime, I got to bury three dead bodies and try to find the next of kin. I'll send some letters to other jurisdictions."

"I don't envy you."

Four men and a middle-aged woman were waiting to board the eastbound stage when it pulled up in front of the hotel. Pettigrew stowed his saddle and gear in the boot at the back of the coach, then helped lift the woman's steamer trunk up to where the teamster and hostler could get hold of it and pull it up on top. Three men sat on one of the two seats while a gent in a fingerlength coat and a homburg hat occupied the other seat with the woman. Pettigrew didn't like riding backward, but the woman got first choice. He took what was left.

With a "Heeyup thar," four horses leaned into their collars and the coach was rolling.

"Say, ain't you—yeah, you're the one that . . . are you the one?" The man cramped beside Pettigrew wore

111

miner's clothes, and was looking him in the face.

Inwardly, Pettigrew groaned. How many times would he have to tell about it? Forcing a wry grin, he answered. "I can guess what you mean, and yeah, I'm him."

Four pairs of eyes were on him, expectantly. He told the story but left out some of the details — he didn't mention catching some buckshot himself, and he didn't mention that one of the dead men was a deputy sheriff gone bad.

"That poor woman. I knew a woman once that was kidnapped by Indians, and she almost died. Not from bein' shot or anything, but just from bein' abused by them red devils."

The woman passenger asked, "Is she . . . is she all right? Did they, uh, you know . . . is she *all right?*"

"I think she's all right," he answered. "I don't think they bothered her. She's a lady of refinement, but she seems to be pretty strong."

"Horrible," the woman said. "Just horrible. I thought now that Colorado's joined the Union there wouldn't be so much shootin' and killin' and robbin'."

With a sad shake of his head, Pettigrew said, "Human nature being what it is, ma'am, I doubt there will ever be an end to that."

"I agree," said the gent seated beside the woman. He pulled back his long coat to reveal a pearl-handled pistol in a holster on his right side. "That's why I never go anywhere without a weapon."

"Guns." The woman spoke harshly. "Too many guns. Guns kill folks."

"I'm not very smart, but I always thought it was the folks who pulled the triggers that were responsible for the killing." With that Pettigrew leaned his head back and tipped his hat over his eyes, ending the conversation.

Were it not for a wooden water tank on high steel legs and a huge pile of coal near the tracks, the train from Trinidad wouldn't have stopped at Yucca. The big engine hissed and steamed while two men in bib overalls climbed to the top of the tank, wrestled with a big hose and filled the boiler with water. Two more railroaders shoveled coal into a compartment behind the boiler. In twenty minutes, the train was rolling again.

There were four gondola cars carrying coal from the mines at Trinidad, two flat cars loaded with bricks and a passenger car. The five passengers from Rosita bought tickets from the conductor.

While the passenger car swayed and rattled, Pettigrew watched the scenery roll by. The bench seat was hard, but this was more comfortable than a stagecoach, and he had more elbow room next to the window. Seated on the east side, he saw the country change from flat desert to rolling hills and back to desert again. They passed a huge cinder cone that looked to be man-made. But no one believed that men—not even the ancient Indians—could stack rocks that high. Pettigrew had heard that the cone grew from a fissure in the earth where thousands of years ago lava bubbled out and piled up.

It was a pleasant journey. Pettigrew smiled inwardly thinking about the things he could do with the reward. Buy a horse-drawn hay mower and a rake—that was one of the first things. Buy a few more saddle horses, and maybe even hire somebody to help him put up hay and round up his cattle and get them down on the winter grass. Fix up the cabin. Rechink the walls where the old mortar had weathered out. It was pleasant thinking of ways to spend money instead of trying to figure out how to get along without it. Five thousand dollars was a lot of money. Maybe he could even buy more patented land. The free range would come to an end some day, probably sooner than folks thought.

It was early night when the train tooted, hissed and

squealed its way into Pueblo. The first thing he did was buy a newspaper from a vendor in the depot. Standing, turning pages, his stomach suddenly went hollow. Mr. Charles B. Atkinson had died from his wounds. The story went on to tell about how Mr. Atkinson and Sheriff Jack Watson of Canon City had been engaged in a gun battle with a gang of kidnappers who held Mr. Atkinson's wife. The sheriff was shot down on the spot and Mr. Atkinson was shot in the stomach. He'd lived long enough to be brought to a hospital in Pueblo, but died in surgery.

It was a sad story. Pettigrew was depressed. He decided not to bother Mrs. Atkinson that time of night. He could wait until morning for his reward. In a room in a working man's hotel, he pulled off the new Levi's and unwrapped his left leg. The wounds had scabbed over and were healing. He rewrapped the leg, not wanting the rough denim pants to rub it raw. After a steak supper in a clean restaurant, he took a bath in the men's water closet and crawled between two clean sheets.

His thoughts went to Mrs. Atkinson, a widow in mourning. She'd survived hell only to learn that her husband was dead. He wished he didn't have to bother her. Maybe he'd spend the last of his money and buy some good wool pants before he went to see her. A man visiting a new widow ought to look his best.

In the lobby of the finest hotel in Pueblo he was told that the widow Atkinson was taking breakfast in her room and did not wish to receive visitors. Pettigrew sent his name upstairs with a clerk, then sat in the lobby and waited. And waited. At mid-morning the clerk approached him.

"Ahem, Mr. Pettigrew?"

Pettigrew looked up. "Yeah?"

"Mrs. Atkinson will see you now."

She was dressed in black. Black silk. Silk with ruffles around the throat, down the front and at the sleeves.

Her red hair had been brushed until it shone. She wore only a touch of lip rouge, and her brown eyes were clear. "Mr. Pettigrew," she smiled a tentative smile. "How nice to see you again. I trust you were not treated too badly at, uh, what is the name of that place?"

"Rosita, ma'am. It's good to see you, too. I'm sure sorry about your husband's death."

"Thank you for your concern. He was a fine man. May I offer you some coffee?"

Pettigrew had been in this room before, but he was still amazed at the opulence. The four-poster bed was covered with a silken quilt. Hand-carved wooden chairs surrounded an oak table, and in a corner stood a tall armoire. A thick carpet covered all but the outer edges of the floor. There was a private water closet. A silver teapot and two china cups sat on the table.

There was also a big cedar chest, open, half-full of folded women's clothing.

"No thanks, Mrs. Atkinson." He stood with his hat in his hands, turning the brim nervously. "I, uh, I hate to bring this up, but, uh, your husband promised a reward to anybody that, uh, brought you back alive."

"Oh, I see." She turned her back to him, long silk robe swirling around her ankles, went to the window, looked out, and turned back to face him. "You certainly have earned it, Mr. Pettigrew, but . . ." Her voice trailed off, and she looked at the carpet.

"Is something wrong?" His heart was climbing into his throat.

"Yes. I'm afraid there is." She looked up, almost in tears. "You see, Mr. Pettigrew, I have no money."

Chapter Sixteen

It had to be a bad dream. Dumbfounded, Pettigrew stammered, "Why, uh, I—I don't understand." He was sick. He thought his knees were going to buckle.

"Sit down, please, Mr. Pettigrew. Let me explain."

Glad to be off his feet, he sat on one of the hand-carved chairs at the oak table. His mind was racing. His stomach was turning flip-flops. She sat across the table from him.

"It's all so . . . complex," she began. "I hardly know where to start."

He waited for her to go on, wishing his stomach would settle down.

"To put it bluntly, we—Charles and I—were never married."

All he could say was, "Huh?"

"Not legally. His wife was impossible to live with and he left her—well-fixed, mind you. He wanted a divorce, but she contested it." Mrs. Atkinson paused, then said, "I apologize for telling you all this, but I want you to understand."

Pettigrew swallowed a lump in his throat.

"Shall I go on?"

"Yeah . . . yes."

"Well, rather than let her and her lawyer take everything, he engaged an attorney too. That was two years ago, Mr. Pettigrew, and the divorce still has not been settled. Charles moved into an apartment near the

116

Loop in Chicago. He was a despondent and lonely man. When I entered his life a year ago I filled the void. A void that badly needed filling. Charles was happy again. We were both happy.

"But," Mrs. Atkinson was clasping and unclasping her hands, "we couldn't marry until the divorce was final. That was why we came West and Charles invested so heavily in the Atchison, Topeka and Santa Fe. We simply had to get away from the snobs who thought our arrangement was a disgrace. We were planning to make Colorado our home."

He understood now. She hadn't fed him all the details, but he got the picture.

"Well, uh, don't you get to keep the, uh, ransom money?"

She shook her head. "I was hoping to, but his wife's lawyer engaged a lawyer here to tie up everything Charles owned. Somehow he found out about the ransom. Just yesterday he showed up with Sheriff Bowen and a court order attaching everything, including the money."

Pettigrew's brain had stopped whirling. He nodded.

"Oh," she exclaimed, spitting out words now, "they were generous. They allowed me to keep my personal belongings and a pittance to live on. So damnably generous."

For the moment, Pettigrew forgot his own problems. "What are you going to do, Mrs. Atkinson?"

A weak smile briefly turned up the corners of her mouth. "Thank you for calling me that. I'm going back to Chicago and find myself a good lawyer. I was Charles' common-law wife, and that ought to count for something. I was more of a wife to him than that bitch ever was, if you'll excuse my language."

"Well." He stood, feeling old and feeble. "Mr. Atkinson promised a reward, but he didn't put it in writing. I have no contract."

"I'm sorry, Mr. Pettigrew. I owe you my life." She put her face in her hands. Her voice was muffled. "I'm so very sorry."

Lem Pettigrew left, closing the door softly behind him.

At first he didn't realize he was mumbling to himself. "Why in hell did old Atkinson have to get himself killed? Just bad luck. God damn bad luck."

Then he was embarrassed. People on the sidewalks of Pueblo were staring at him, stepping wide around him. He ducked into the Arkansaw Saloon, went up to the bar. Without even looking at the other patrons he ordered a beer, then another, then a shot of whiskey. The whiskey burned its way down his throat and into his stomach, but it felt good. It helped clear his mind, helped him to think.

"All right, all right," he mumbled.

"What say?"

"Oh, uh, nothing," Pettigrew said to a well-dressed man standing at the bar beside him. He ordered another mug of beer and sipped instead of guzzled. He tried to force himself to forget the whole thing. Forget the buckshot wounds in his left leg, forget the shootout in the Sierra Mojadas, forget the shootout in a hotel room in Rosita, and most important of all, forget Mrs. Cynthia Atkinson, whoever she really was. She was beautiful, he admitted to himself. The way she looked a few minutes ago in those silky female clothes, hair brushed, face clean, brought back feelings he had been fighting for years.

Aw hell, just forget her and concentrate on the problems at home.

Home. No money, short another horse, damn few groceries. He might shoot a deer for meat. That and a bushel of potatoes would keep him eating as long as the meat stayed fresh. When it spoiled, he'd shoot another deer. But he had to have

118

more than that. Maybe he'd sell some beef.

Hell! Damn! He wanted his herd to grow, not shrink. But a man's got to eat. Come to think of it, what would he shoot a buckskin with? He'd left his Winchester up in the foothills near Hardscrabble. He'd have to get awfully close to a deer to kill it with his Colt .45. Or maybe he could do like Beans Gipson did and steal a few head of cattle. Naw, that wouldn't do.

Well, first he had to get home, and that wouldn't be easy. He pulled his wallet out of a shirt pocket and counted his money. He didn't know whether he had enough to buy a stage ticket to Canon City. It would be better if he could catch a ride on a freight wagon. Had to check out of that hotel before they charged him for another night. Had to get home with at least a few dollars in his pockets. He sure couldn't afford to stand here and drink all day.

Pettigrew carried his saddle, saddlebags and blanket roll to the stage company's barn. He soon learned that he could buy a ticket, but it would take most of the few dollars he had left. Could he work his way?

"Weel now." The stage line owner, a man named Jameson, rubbed a whiskered jaw, studied the ground, studied Pettigrew. "Tell yu, son, I'm sendin' four wagon loads of groceries over there. We'll start loadin' in about an hour, and we'll get to Canon City just before daylight — like to haul freight at night while it's cool. If you wanta help load them wagons, I'll see ya git a seat on one of 'em."

Pettigrew worked most of the afternoon and rode a wagon seat all night. While he rode, trying to stay awake and keep from falling off, his mind drifted back over everything that had happened and Mrs. Cynthia Atkinson. Something about her that had tugged at his mind before was tugging again.

119

Aw hell, Lem Pettigrew he mused to himself, you're tired, sleepy, and not thinking straight.

At Canon City he helped unload the wagons and was paid enough to buy his breakfast. After a meal of hot cakes with no meat, he stashed his saddle in the freight office and started walking.

It never seemed like any distance at all when he was horseback or in a wagon, but walking made it seem like fifty miles instead of four or five. He was tired, discouraged and disgusted with the world. Put one foot in front of the other. Keep going. His left leg was giving him only a little discomfort now. He was thankful for that, but he was worried too.

His first problem when he got home would be catching one of his horses. With no fences to hold them they could be ten miles away, and they weren't about to let a man on foot walk up to them. If he had some grain to use as a bribe, the bell mare might let him catch her. She was a gentle old girl, but if the other horses ran she'd run with them. And even if he could catch one he'd have to ride bareback to town to get his saddle and stuff. He'd be damned if he was going to try to wrangle horses into a corral riding bareback.

Put one foot in front of the other.

There was no bridge across Cripple Creek. The creek was never more than hock deep to a horse along here. He'd ridden across it a hundred times, but never waded across. Should he pull off his boots? Hell no. He'd walked in his sock feet enough up there in the Mojadas, sneaking up on sleeping men. Let his boots get wet. They'd dry. Walk.

As he walked he grumbled to himself, "Left here on a good horse and come back walking. A man on foot was nothing. A man on foot couldn't catch a hobbled pissant. Man wasn't made for walking. Even the Indians didn't walk. Aw hell, Lem Pettigrew, shut up and walk. One foot in front of the other.

His boots were squishing water by the time he got across the creek. Let them squish. He'd give every dollar in his pocket to see his horses grazing near the cabin. He stopped and listened for the bell mare. No such luck. Well, get home, get his one extra bridle, then go horse hunting and horse chasing — on foot.

Pettigrew was still grumbling to himself when he came in sight of the cabin. Suddenly he stopped. He dragged a shirt sleeve across his eyes. He blinked, shook his head and stared. It couldn't be.

The first thing he noticed was smoke coming out of the chimney. Naw. His brain wasn't working right. And was that a horse in the corral? Naw. He wiped his eyes again.

Yeah, there was somebody in the cabin and a horse in the corral. He had a visitor. "Who in hell . . . ?" he said out loud. Whoever it was had been there all night. The horse was munching on hay. Pettigrew's meager supply of hay. Somdamnbody was making himself at home. Probably eating Pettigrew's meager supply of groceries too.

Was he friendly? Or was Pettigrew in somebody's gunsights?

"Well, by God . . . he spat, "that's my house and I'll be damned if I'm gonna let anydamnbody keep me out of it."

He drew the Colt .45, checked the loads. Five in the cylinder, an empty under the hammer. He cocked the hammer back, watched the cylinder turn to put a live cartridge in place, then walked, eyes wary.

He watched the window and the door. Any movement at all and he'd hit the ground. When he crossed the open yard between the corral and the cabin, he was afraid to blink. Now he was at the door. Whoever was in there surely knew he was coming. Either saw him, or heard him, or both — waiting behind the door for him to step inside.

Gripping the Colt, ready to shoot, he put his left hand on the latch. He'd shove the door open and step back. See what happened.

He shoved the door so hard it slammed against the inside wall, stepped back. Nothing happened. He yelled, "Come out of there." No answer. Somebody was waiting for him to show himself in the door. "Who's in there?" he yelled again. "Come out."

Oh lord, Pettigrew muttered under his breath. Now what? Well, he'd have to risk it. Whoever it was was either behind the door or in the other room. The thing to do was jump inside, but not far enough for a man behind the door to see him. Jump to where he could see the doorway to the bedroom. Shoot fast and straight. Ready, go.

In two long quick steps he was through the door, eyes darting from the kitchen to the bedroom door and back to the kitchen. He immediately picked out the man sitting at the table. The man was sitting relaxed with the chair tilted back on its hind legs. His hands were behind his head, fingers laced. He wore a big smile.

"Howdy, partner," said John "Beans" Gipson.

Chapter Seventeen

Pettigrew could only stammer. "What . . . ? Beans, what in holy hell . . . ?"

The young cowboy's smile widened. "Surprised? How come? Didn't you get my letter?"

"Yeah, but I didn't think you'd—what're you doing here?" Pettigrew still stood in the open door. He let his gun hand drop to his side.

"Wa-al," Beans Gipson drawled, ". . . as I recomember, we had some unfinished business."

Pettigrew's eyes narrowed. His nerves were alert, ready for trouble. The young man was wearing a walnut-handled sixgun in a holster on his right side. But he was still relaxed, still tilted back, still smiling.

Pettigrew asked, "Did you come here looking for revenge or something?"

"Well, partner, whatta you think? Think I oughta be lookin' for revenge?"

"I don't know. Are you?"

"What would you do if you was me?"

"If I was you? Well, if I was you I'd be the last man I'd want to see." Pettigrew paused, thinking. "To tell the truth, if I was you I'd be pretty damned mad at my ex-partner, but not mad enough to kill anybody."

"I ain't here to kill nobody. If I was I coulda dropped you out there in the yard."

"Then what do you want?"

"I'm not real sure, partner. Have some java. How come you ain't got no coffee pot? How come you're walkin'? Where'n the humped-up world you been, anyways?"

For the first time since he'd entered the cabin, Pettigrew smelled coffee. It smelled good. "You sure you're not here to get even?"

"Give you my word I ain't here to shoot nobody. Gettin' even? I dunno. Ain't decided what to do about that. Relax. I had to boil coffee in a pan, but it ain't too bad. Set. I'll pour you a cup."

With a relieved sigh, Pettigrew let the hammer down on the Colt and holstered it. He pulled out the one other chair in the room and sat. Beans Gipson stood and went to the stove where coffee was simmering in a tin pan. "Had no trouble findin' you. First one I ast was a purty girl at the post office. She knowed right away who I was askin' about, and told me how to get here. She ever been here, partner?"

"No, but she knows where I live and all."

"You sweet on her?"

"Yeah, some, but you still haven't told me what you're doing here."

"Tell ya in a minute. Pour some of this coffee down ya." Beans Gipson filled a tin cup and set it on the table in front of Pettigrew. "You et this mornin'?"

"Yeah, a little. I'm not hungry yet."

The young cowboy poured himself a cup of coffee and sat across the table. His hat was tilted back, revealing a hank of dark thick hair curled over his forehead. His blue eyes crinkled at the edges when he smiled a handsome smile. Pettigrew remembered him as a young man who smiled a lot.

"Somethin' tells me, partner, you got a story to tell. Here you come afoot, lookin' like a old horse with the colic. You're almost out of chuck, and I'll bet you ain't got two nickels to rub together."

Grinning a wry grin, Pettigrew said, "How'd you guess?"

Beans Gipson tilted his chair back on its hind legs again, and said, "I ain't heard a good story in a long time. Tell me about it."

Pettigrew sipped hot coffee and told the story for the umpteenth time, hitting only the high spots. Beans Gipson's smile faded when Pettigrew told about the shooting and the killing. By the time Pettigrew finished talking the coffee was cold. He got up, pried a lid off the stove and stirred the ashes. He put the coffee pan over the open hole.

"I've got a coffee pot rolled up in my blankets," he said. "I left my saddle and everything at the freight office."

"Well, I'll run in your horses for ya." Beans shook his head. "If I counted right you killed four men."

"Yeah." Pettigrew sighed. "Four."

"All for a reward that you didn't get."

"Well, they tried to kill me."

"Yeah, but you didn't get a nickel out of it."

"Not a red cent."

"Damnedest story I ever heard. Me, I ain't always been on the right side of the law, but I never killed nobody."

"Have you ever been shot at?"

"No. Well, yeah, once. But I outrun the bullets. I didn't know the damn woman had a husband. Tell ya, though, I was ready to shoot a Mexican ranchero a few days ago. I shoved this sixgun up his nose and was ready to pull the trigger if he didn't pay me."

Pettigrew put a stick of firewood in the stove. "Why was that?"

"Well, if you re'clect, them beefs we stole was drove across the Rio Grande before you c'd get the shurff."

Not wanting to be reminded of that, Pettigrew said nothing.

"Fact is, they never did pay us for 'em. So a few days ago, right after I got out, I went for a visit across the border. I got our money."

"Not our money. Yours maybe."

The smile was back. "Suit yourself. But it looks to me like you could sure use a few bucks. If ol' Lady Luck gave me a kick in the ass like she just did you, I'd take anything I c'd get."

"This damned coffee ain't gonna amount to anything. Sure, I could use a few bucks. But I won't starve."

Standing, pulling his hat down, Beans said, "I'll go jangle for ya. You better go in there and lay down before you fall over. How come you didn't take your bed tarp and mattress with you?"

"I would have had to take a pack horse, and two horses make more noise than one. And why would you do anything for me?"

The smile faded, then returned. "Damned if I know. I'm a booger for punishment, I reckon."

Another bed was rolled out on the floor in the bedroom. It was a cowboy bedroll, with a long tarp under it, folded back over a thin mattress and some blankets, the same kind of bed Pettigrew had on his bunk. He pulled off his boots and lay on his bed without getting under the tarp. How long had Beans Gipson been here, he wondered. And why did he come here? He slept until he heard boots thumping on the floor in the kitchen. He went to the connecting door in his sock feet, thin brown hair sticking out in all directions.

Beans said, "We're gonna have to get some chuck when we go after your saddle and stuff. I mixed a batch of flapjack dough this mornin', and I reckon that's what we'll have for dinner. I see a can of beans we can heat up and spread over 'em."

"Whatta ya mean we? You lousy?"

126

At that Beans chuckled. "Not that I know of. I been thinkin', partner. I been thinkin' all the time I rode up here. I didn't know whether to be fightin' mad or what. But when I seen how poor you are and how Lady Luck has shit on you, I decided I ain't fightin' mad. And I ain't got nothin' else to do, so I reckon I'll he'p you gather your cattle."

"I could use some help, but how do you think I'm gonna pay you? Or feed you?"

"I'm rich. Hog rich, anyways. That Mex ranchero shelled out a hunnerd and fifty bucks. If you don't want any of it, I'll bet you'll be happy to eat some of the chuck it'll buy."

Grinning, running his fingers through his hair, Pettigrew said, "You're right. I guess we'd better take the wagon to town. How far away were the horses?"

"Four, five miles east. I figgered they wouldn't be too far from water."

"They ought to be well rested, but I need more. There's a hell of a lot of country up there to ride."

"I've got two. I've been packin' my bed on one, but he ain't a bad saddle horse. He's staked out over yonder by the creek."

The meal was filling, but not the sort of food a man would want to live on. Pettigrew harnessed his team and hitched them to the wagon. Beans turned his two horses out with Pettigrew's and climbed up on the wagon seat. "These ol' ponies stake broke?"

"Yeah," Pettigrew answered. "They all are. The only trouble around here is finding enough grass out away from the trees where they don't get their picket ropes wrapped around anything. They feed better running loose."

"Don't they all."

Nodding to the north, Pettigrew said, "Up there in the high hills there are spots where the grass is stirrup high and a horse can graze all summer."

127

"I figgered your cattle are summerin' up there. How many cows you got?"

The two talked on the way to town, but neither mentioned the cattle stealing they'd done together, nor the way it had ended. Beans didn't mention the Texas prison, and Pettigrew didn't want to ask. He considered telling Beans how badly he felt about ratting on him, but decided to keep it to himself.

They tied the team to a hitching post in front of the Canon City Mercantile, and Pettigrew said, "It's your money, so you decide what to buy. I'm going visiting for a few minutes."

"That gal at the post office?"

"Yup."

"She's a purty one."

Betsy was all smiles the second he walked through the door. Her brown hair was parted on the side, and a blue ribbon was tied from back to front. It matched her blue dress. And her eyes. Pettigrew wanted to take her in his arms and kiss her, but there was no privacy in the one-room post office. All they could do was smile at each other.

"A fella was here looking for you yesterday. I told him where to find your place. I hope he was a friend."

"Yeah, he's over at the store. I think he's planning on staying around a while and helping me find my cattle."

"He's good looking."

"I guess he is. I never noticed."

"When are you coming over for supper? How about tonight?"

"Well, not tonight, but will tomorrow night do?"

She squeezed his arm. "Any night will do."

Back at the mercantile, Beans and the storekeeper, wearing a long white apron, were carrying groceries out to the wagon. When they were finished, Pettigrew said, "You durn near got a wagon load."

"Yep. Lessee, now, I got beans, spuds, onions, some dried fruit, flour, yeast powder, coffee, sugar, salt, a can of lard and a can of molasses, ten pounds of bacon, and, oh yeah, a twenty-five pound bag of oats. That's to make the horses easier to catch. I'll bet that bell mare of yours will come up and eat out of your hand."

"God damn, Beans, you bought out the store. How in hell am I gonna pay you back?"

"I'll let you worry about that. I ain't a-goin' to."

Pettigrew did his laundry before dark. He heated some water, half-filled his wash tub and dumped in a handful of soap. He used a clothes stomper, which resembled an inverted tin funnel with a long handle, to work the clothes up and down in the tub. Rinsing was done in the creek. The duds were hung on tree limbs to dry.

Supper was a bachelor's feast: cowboy biscuits baked in the oven, dried fruit, and boiled potatoes covered with red sop, which Beans made by browning flour in bacon fat and adding water. "We're gonna have to go huntin', partner. Beef costs too much. There's gotta be some buckskins up in them hills."

Pettigrew leaned back in his chair, patted his stomach and grinned. "I lost my rifle. How good a shot are you with that hogleg pistol of yours?"

"Me and this old forty-some-odd have brought home meat before."

They went hunting, but all they brought back were two cottontail rabbits. They agreed they'd take a pack horse and their bedrolls and go farther up in the hills. "But," said Beans, "these cottontails are better'n Texas jackrabbits. Ever eat a jackrabbit, Lem?"

"Tried to. Once. I'd as soon starve."

"Feller's gotta be purty hungry to eat a jackrabbit."

"Well, you can cook yourself some of your favorite beans tonight and have some fried rabbit with them.

Me, I'm gonna go calling and have a woman-cooked meal."

"That gal at the post office?"

"Yup."

"Your luck ain't all bad, after all," Beans drawled.

Riding down the main street of Canon City that evening, Pettigrew decided Beans was right. His luck could have been worse. He knew when he went after the reward he was asking for trouble. And how could he have been so lucky as to find a doctor at Hardscrabble? And then there was Betsy. A fine woman. Pretty. Besides, he was freshly shaved, bathed and was wearing clean clothes. Yeah, things could have been worse. Then he heard his name called.

"Pettigrew. Lemual Pettigrew." It was a man's voice, demanding, full of authority.

Pettigrew's head swiveled to the left. A tall, thin man with a hawk-like face and slits for eyes stood on the boardwalk. He wore a sixgun in a low holster and a silver star on his shirt.

"Yeah?" Pettigrew reined up.

"You're Lemual Pettigrew, ain't you?"

"I am."

"I'm Marshal Dodds, a United States Marshal, and I'm investigating the murder of Sheriff Watson and his deputy. I understand you had somethin' to do with that."

Sensing trouble, Pettigrew answered guardedly, "Yeah."

"Get down off that horse and come with me. I want some answers from you, and I want 'em straight."

"Well, right now I've got something else to do."

"I don't give a damn what you've got to do. When I say come with me, you come with me."

Pettigrew stepped down and faced the marshal. A few pedestrians had stopped to see what was going to happen. Heat was building in Pettigrew's neck and face. His heart was beating too fast. He spoke slowly, but with strength: "And when I say I've got something else to do, I mean I've got something else to do."

Chapter Eighteen

They faced each other. Both men stood spraddle-legged, right hands near their gun butts. The marshal was on the plank walk in front of a hardware store, Pettigrew stood in the street. They were so close neither man could miss. Pedestrians gathered, but stayed back. No one spoke.

Pettigrew knew the kind—a lawman so full of authority he couldn't contain it. When he hollered, citizens were supposed to jump. Pettigrew was holding reins in his left hand. When the horse moved nervously, he dropped the reins, not wanting the horse to distract his attention. He knew he couldn't win. The marshal could kill him and it would be in the line of duty. The way it would be told, the marshal had put his life on the line to protect the citizens from a criminal. If he killed the marshal he'd be hung for murder. He'd be the criminal.

But Pettigrew had already spent some time in jail for rescuing a kidnapped woman. He'd answered a hundred questions from a deputy sheriff, a coroner's jury and a sheriff.

Finally, the marshal spoke through tight lips, "I ain't put you under arrest yet, but I'm about to."

"To hell with you and your arrest."

"All right—you're under arrest. Are you gonna resist arrest?"

"Damn right."

The marshal was a gunfighter. He carried his six-gun low, near his right hand. The trigger guard was exposed, so all he had to do was raise his hand and the gun would be in it. His finger would be on the trigger. Pettigrew knew how to do it. He'd practiced the fast draw as a deputy in Texas, but now his gun was deeper in its holster where it wouldn't fall out accidentally. And he was out of practice. Rusty. He watched the marshal's eyes and concentrated on his own gun hand.

It was quiet on the street of Canon City. The air was full of tension. Onlookers scarcely breathed. Somebody was about to be killed.

Then the door behind the marshal opened. Opened outwardly. A man stepped out, settling a homburg hat on his head, looking down. He collided with the marshal. "Whup. Sorry."

"Sorry, hell." The marshal turned his slitted eyes toward the owner of the hardware store. His hawk-like face was purple with anger. "Why in hell don't you look where you're goin'?"

The store owner stopped short. "I was just . . . uh, I'm gonna fix that door so it opens the other way. I didn't mean to—"

"I oughtta arrest you for interferin' with an officer of the law. I oughtta haul you to the hoosegow right now. I oughtta—"

"He didn't mean nothin', Marshal." It was a bearded miner who spoke. "He was just tryin' to go on about his business."

"That's the way of it," another onlooker said. "He didn't do nothin' wrong."

"'Course," another put in, "ol' Tobe oughtta fix that dang door. I almost got knocked over by it oncet."

"Hey, Tobe, you oughtta put a bell on that door.

Or blow a whistle or somethin'."

Someone chuckled. "Yeah, toot a whistle before he opens 'er, so ever'body'll know to stand back."

"I learnt a long time ago to step wide around ol' Tobe's door."

Another chuckle. "Seen a drummer walk by here oncet with a fat cigar in his face. Next he knowed, ol' Tobe's door opened and he was wearin' that see-gar."

"Haw-haw. I seen a woman beat 'im over the head with her umbreller fer almost hittin' 'er with that door."

Laughter. "Hey, Tobe, how many times you gonna get beat up by women before you fix that dadgummed door?"

Tobe sputtered. "Why, why, I'll change it tomorra. I promise I will. I swear I will."

Men were moving, joking, hoorawing Tobe. The marshal and Pettigrew were forgotten. "First thing you gotta do, Tobe, is sharpen them durned tools you sell."

"Ever' time he sells a cuttin' tool he's gotta sell a grindstone to go with it."

Pettigrew stepped closer to the marshal. "All right, I'll go to the sheriff's office or wherever you want and I'll answer your questions. But I'm keeping my gun and I ain't going to jail."

The marshal was flustered. He said, "You'll do what I . . ." He stopped in mid-sentence. His shoulders sagged a little. Only a little, and he immediately squared them. But when he spoke again, his voice wasn't so full of authority. "I hear you've killed four men, and the U.S. government don't take kindly to that. As long as you cooperate—if your story checks—but I'm gonna do a lot of checking, and if you try to leave the territory I'll be right after you."

Betsy wasn't smiling. "Your supper is cold," she said, standing with her hands on her hips. "The stove is cold. You can eat a cold supper or go hungry."

Pettigrew felt like a spanked puppy. "I, uh, something happened. I was on my way, only a few blocks from here, and . . ."

She didn't let him finish. "Eat if you want to but whatever you do, do it quick. I'm going to bed." She spun and stomped across the room, stopped and spun back. "Alone."

"I'm sorry." He stood with his hat in his hands. "I mean it. I don't say that very often."

She glared at him, then pulled out a chair and sat at the table. "What happened?"

With a sigh, Pettigrew asked, "Mind if I sit down?"

"No. I'm not sure I want you to sit."

"Well." He shifted his weight from one foot to the other. "I guess I have got a lot of explaining to do. Where can I start? Well, you've heard about the woman being kidnapped, Mrs. Atkinson?" He turned his hat in his hands. "Well, her husband offered a reward, and I need the money, and I . . . well, I had to track kidnappers plumb over the Mojadas, but I rescued her."

That got a small reaction. Betsy's face softened, and she said, "I heard something about that. Sit down."

Sitting, holding his hat in his lap, Pettigrew went on. "I didn't get the reward. Mr. Atkinson was killed. Him and Sheriff Watson. It was their killers that I tracked over the Mojadas. One of them was his deputy, Ellsworth. It was Mr. Atkinson who offered the reward, but with him dead, I won't get it."

135

Betsy's grey eyes were holding his, forcing him to look down. "I . . . you'll hear about it sooner or later. I've killed four men." He added quickly, "I didn't set out to kill anybody. All I wanted to do was rescue that woman and claim the reward. It — it's just the way things turned out."

They were silent. Then Betsy said softly, "I thought you were such a gentleman, Lem. Quiet. Polite. You've always carried a gun, but so does nearly everyone else. I didn't think you had it in you to kill four men."

"I didn't think so either."

Again they were silent, and again it was Betsy who broke the silence. "I want you to go, Lem. I need to think about this. Right now I don't know what to think."

Standing, he said, "I wish it hadn't happened. I'll go."

"Wait. I almost forgot. Here's a letter for you." She took the envelope off a shelf and handed it to him. Without looking at it he folded it and put it in his shirt pocket.

Riding out of town in the light of a half-moon, Pettigrew's thoughts were sad. Sad and then bitter. "God damn it," he said aloud, "she didn't let me explain why I was late for supper."

Pettigrew and Beans Gipson spent the next five days riding. They left on a high trot each morning at daylight, heading up into the timbered hills. It took that long to locate fifty-four cows and their calves and three of the bulls. They looked for bony longhorn cattle wearing Pettigrew's Rafter 4 brand with an underslope cut in the left ear.

Beans shot a young buck deer with velvety antlers. Dressed out it went home with them on the back of a saddle. They had fresh meat.

"What," Beans had asked once, "if we see some grown cattle that ain't branded?"

"They're not mine," Pettigrew said. "I lived with my cows at calving time and again in the early summer. I slept and ate with them. I didn't miss anything. Mine are all branded."

"If you don't slap your iron on 'em somebody else will."

"That's their business. What I would like to see is somebody else's bulls servicing my cows. I could use some good bulls."

"Yup. I seen a big ol' red bull yesterday that's packin' a lot of beef. He was wearin' a brand that looked like a slash J. I don't know how an animal like that will winter, but he's sure fat now and lookin' for somethin' to stick his diddly in."

"Don't move him out of his tracks, but if you happen to see some of my bony cows anywhere near, make sure he sees them or smells them."

Grinning, Beans said, "Yeah, a damn animal don't care what a female looks like as long as she's in heat."

"All I want to do now is get my stuff together and keep them from drifting out of the high country too soon."

Pettigrew changed shirts that night, putting on the shirt he'd worn the last time he was in town. It was then that he found the letter, the one Betsy had given him. With everything else on his mind, he had forgotten about it. It was addressed to Lemual Petagru, Canyon City, Colorada. He tore the envelope open and read:

I know yur name and where yu live. Yu are dead. It was not signed.

"Aw for . . . now what?" Pettigrew said aloud.

Beans was living up to his nickname, cooking beans. "What're you mumblin' about?"

"Read this." Pettigrew handed him the letter. Beans read it.

"Somebody don't like you, partner. Any idee who wrote this?"

With a sigh, Pettigrew said, "No, not offhand. I can't think of anybody that would want to kill me. Unless it's one of the two that tried to kill me in my hotel room in Rosita. The one that got away. Must be him."

"Wal, you shot three of his partners and snatched a lot of money from under their noses."

"He wouldn't be so dumb as to be looking for revenge."

"He might be." A wry grin touched Beans' face. "I thought about it. I reckon he c'd be thinkin' about it, too."

"He'd have nothing to gain, but . . ." Pettigrew studied the floor and rubbed his jaw. "I can't think of anybody else."

"Think he means it?"

"I don't know." Still rubbing his jaw, Pettigrew added, "This place could be mighty unhealthy, Beans. I almost got bushwhacked here once. The next time I might not be so lucky. Maybe you oughtta ride out."

"That does make it kinda uncomfortable around here, don't it? The way I see it the only place a bushwhacker can hide is in them trees and weeds by the crik. What we have to do is go out the bedroom window ever' mornin' and circle to where we can get behind 'em."

"This ain't your problem."

The wry grin returned. "I usta think I was comin' here for revenge, and now there's some-body else lookin' for revenge. Partner, you got

138

a way of makin' friends."

"It's been five days since I got this letter. We were in danger and didn't know it. Maybe he won't show."

Beans changed the subject. "Takes too damn long to cook anything up here. These musical fruits've been cookin' for two hours and they ain't done yet."

"The air is thinner here than it is in south Texas. It takes longer to boil anything."

They said no more about the threat, but when they got up in the mornings they took a long look out each window, then slipped out the bedroom window one at a time and got behind the loafing shed. From there they studied the weeds and trees before going any farther.

In four more days they had worn down five horses and still hadn't located all of Pettigrew's cattle. He decided he'd take a fresh horse and a pack horse and camp up in the mountains for two or three days. "I'm gonna take my bed and plenty of groceries," he said. "We've been all over the Red Canyon country and plumb up to Fourmile Canyon. I believe I'll get on the other side of Cooper Mountain, along Phantom Canyon. If I find anything I'll push them over to Garden Park."

"What some help?"

"Naw. We're short of horses. Besides, I can't pay you. You oughtta go to town. Don't take any chances on being bushwhacked. Go to town and take it easy."

"That feller that wrote you the letter, he prob'ly only wanted to scare ya, make ya worry."

"Probably."

"But I'll tell ya, partner, I met a lot of men in the pen, and there's some folks you just can't figure. The ones that don't make no sense are the ones you have to be careful of."

"You're right. That's why I wish you'd get the hell out of here. I don't want to come back and find you dead."

"Maybe I will. I'm sorta in heat myself."

Pettigrew grinned. "What you need, Beans, is a wife. Then you wouldn't have to be always looking for some of that ol' stuff."

"If you know anybody that'd have this ranihan, send 'er around. All I ask is she ain't wore plumb out. And knows how to cook beans. Well, never mind the cookin'. I c'n cook beans as good as any woman."

It rained the day Pettigrew left. Rain in the high country nearly always came with thunder and lightning. Thunder started as a rolling sound far to the west. Lightning zig-zagged on top of Cooper Mountain.

"Looks like we're gonna get wet, fellers," Pettigrew said to his horses. He was riding Rowdy and leading the bell mare. "It'll be worth it, though. Country's too dry. It needs rain to make the grass grow." A few fat drops fell on his shoulders and hat. He got down, untied the long yellow slicker from behind his saddle and put it on. Rowdy didn't like the looks of it, and refused to stand still while Pettigrew got mounted again.

"Whoa, now. Smells like dead fish, but it's harmless." He managed to get his left foot in the stirrup. Rowdy watched him, looking back with eyes made for wide peripheral vision. Pettigrew swung up into the saddle. "Whoa, now. Behave your fool self." Rowdy had a hump in his back for a few steps, then quieted down.

Lightning struck suddenly like the tip of a whip. A granite boulder on Pettigrew's left sizzled. At the same instant thunder split the world apart with a deafening crack. Had Pettigrew not had a long-time

140

habit of always sitting tight in the saddle, Rowdy would have thrown him off.

"God damn," he said. "That was too damned close. Let's find a low spot." He reined the horse downhill where lightning was less likely to strike. But he was riding on granite, and a horse's iron-shod hooves on granite was inviting danger. "Dammit. Where in hell can we go?"

They headed for a pine forest where the ground was covered with pine needles. There, Pettigrew dismounted, hung onto his horses and hunched down in the slicker while hail stones the size of marbles beat on them. The bell mare put her head down, humped her back and prepared to endure. Rowdy danced nervously for a minute, then did the same. Hail soon covered the ground like snow. Next it rained.

Looking at the sky, getting his face wet, Pettigrew allowed the rain was going to last a while. "Well, hell, we've been rained on before," he said. He mounted again, wrapped the pack horse's lead rope once around the saddle horn and put the end under his right thigh. "Let's get on up there."

The cattle trail they were following was an easy one in dry weather. Now it was muddy and covered with white hail stones. They were traveling around a grassy hill that rose steeply on one side of the trail. The terrain on the other side dropped into a deep *arroyo*. Pettigrew could imagine himself in the bottom of that *arroyo* with a horse on top of him.

"Watch where you put them feet down, partner," he said. He'd been a cowboy long enough that it didn't occur to him to walk and lead his horses.

Gradually, the rain slackened. A hole appeared in the clouds to the west, and within thirty minutes, the sun was shining. Grinning to himself, Pettigrew said aloud, "Nobody can predict the weather in this

141

country."

By the time they were north of Cooper Mountain, the hailstones had melted, revealing cow tracks. And there were other tracks—big cat tracks. A cougar.

Chapter Nineteen

Riding on, following cattle tracks, Pettigrew found fifteen of his cows and two bulls in a clearing next to an unnamed creek. Fourteen of the cows had calves, and the calves were growing fast. "I'd hate to rassle these boogers all day," Pettigrew mused. The cows were as fat as longhorns could be, and they were wild, ready to run if the man on a horse got too close. But one spotted cow stood off by herself, lowing softly. Pettigrew rode over, leading his pack horse. He could tell by the drying slobbers around the cow's teats that she'd had a calf.

"Uh-oh," he said aloud. "Looks like she's lost her baby." He rode on, and under a tall ponderosa he found the calf. It was half-eaten. God damn. There's enough mule deer around here that them God damn cats don't have to kill calves. Son of a bitch."

He unloaded the bell mare near the creek and rolled out his bed. He camped within sight of the dead calf's remains, hoping the cougar would come back so he could get a shot at it. With his horses staked out on the tall grass, he gathered enough flat rocks to build a fire on. Though the trees were still wet from the rain, there were enough dead lower branches that he had plenty of firewood. While the rocks heated, he ate cold bread and apple butter, then set a gallon lard can half full of beans on the hot rocks. The granite would hold heat long enough

143

to warm the beans for supper. He saddled the bell mare and went looking for more cattle.

On the rim of Phantom Canyon he found three more cows and their calves. Two of the calves were healthy, but the other was near death. It took only a glance to see why. The animal had gotten too curious about a porcupine, and now had a nose full of quills. It couldn't eat, couldn't suck, and was slowly starving.

Pettigrew took down his catch rope, tied one end hard and fast to his saddle horn and shook out a loop in the other end. "Well, old lady," he said to the mare, "I've never roped off you before. Put me within throwing distance, will you?" He slapped spurs to the mare's sides and took off at a dead run.

The mare responded with surprising speed and was on the calf within seconds. The calf was running its best, but it was no match for the horse. Pettigrew swung the loop over his head to keep it open and to put some power behind it. It was an easy catch.

On the ground, he pulled a pigging string from under the back rigging rings of his saddle, then tied the reins to the rope near the horse's nose. That would keep her from turning around and dragging the calf. He tucked the tie string under his belt and went down the rope.

The calf looked to be weak from hunger, but it jumped and bawled on the end of the rope. Pettigrew got his left arm under its neck and his right hand on its right flank. The calf bawled, jumped and kicked. A sharp hind hoof peeled skin off Pettigrew's right leg. But he kept his hold, and when the calf jumped again, he turned it over in midair and let it fall on its side.

With the calf hogtied, Pettigrew kneeled with one knee behind its right ear to hold its head down while he picked out the quills. "I know it hurts," he said, "but you'll feel better when it's over." The cow was walking in a half-circle nearby, head down, trying to decide whether to attack the man. It took a good fifteen minutes, and Pettigrew wished he'd had some pliers, but working with his fingers and fingernails, he got the quills out. He slipped the rope off the calf's neck, untied its feet and let it up. Mounted, he gathered his rope and watched the calf. It ran a short distance with the cow following at a trot, then stopped, butted the cow in the flank and started sucking. Pettigrew grinned.

He spent the next hour riding along the rim of Phantom Canyon, but saw no more cattle. Tomorrow he'd ride west, along Beaver Creek. Some daylight was left when he returned to his camp, got the mare picketed, and rebuilt the fire. He fried bacon on the reheated rocks and made his meal of bacon and beans.

Stomach full, horses watered and moved to fresh graze, he lay on his back on his bed, looking at the sky. He enjoyed listening to the horses crop the grass, the night breeze. His grin faded when he remembered spending nights in the Mojadas, hurting, hungry, and fearful of what he might find ahead. All for nothing, and it wasn't over. A revenge-seeking gunhand could shoot him in the back at any time, a U.S. marshal was trying to find enough evidence to arrest him for murder. And that woman, Cynthia Atkinson. Some woman. Odd. The whole damned deal was odd. She was like a jigsaw puzzle with pieces that didn't fit.

Thinking about her so occupied Pettigrew's mind that he wasn't aware at first of a strange sound. Gradually, it worked through to his consciousness. It was barely audible, a grinding, crunching. Suddenly, he knew what it was.

Moving slowly, he pulled on his boots and stood,

lifted the Colt .45 from its holster. Trying to walk quietly, he moved in the direction of the dead calf. A three-quarter moon put out enough light that he could see the carcass, see the dark form crouched beside it.

Pettigrew knelt on one knee, rested his right elbow on the upraised knee, grasped his right wrist in his left hand, held his gun hand straight out. Aimed. Fired.

The big cat jumped straight up and fell over backwards. Pettigrew advanced slowly, gun held straight out, ready to shoot again. The cougar had been hit in the hind quarters and couldn't move its hind legs. It was dragging itself with its front feet. Pettigrew aimed and fired another shot, sending a .45 slug into its heart.

"You won't kill another calf," he said.

He started early next morning, gathering the cattle he'd found and driving them across Phantom Canyon. Rowdy worked hard, keeping that many cattle together and moving in the right direction over rough steep country. Pettigrew let the bell mare follow. By noon they were across the canyon. He stopped, unsaddled Rowdy and let him rest and graze, but not for long. When the cattle began to scatter too far he saddled the mare and led Rowdy as he continued, yelling, whistling, and swearing at cattle, moving them east.

He didn't know how far it was to the Garden Park country, but he realized he wasn't going to get there that day. He camped at the edge of a pine forest, ate bacon, cold biscuits and more of Beans Gipson's favorite fruit.

With daylight came more flapjacks, bacon and coffee, and more riding, yelling and whistling, pushing the cattle. It was shortly after noon when he saw some of the cows he and Beans had gathered. He urged his herd on until they came to open country along Cripple Creek. "Eat," he said. "Stay fat, but don't stray too far." Then he turned his horse toward home.

Riding home wasn't a happy trip. He didn't know what he'd find there. He could find a killer, or worse yet, not see him until it was too late. He could find Beans gone, or dead. And he could find a law officer with a warrant for his arrest, hoping he'd resist arrest.

What he found, when he rode up across the creek from his cabin, was a man with a rifle, waiting for him.

Chapter Twenty

Pettigrew had crossed the creek a mile upstream, and was riding down the west side. He stayed as far from the trees and weeds as he could and still be close enough that he could see a man over there—if there was a man over there. He was wary, eyes studying the most likely hiding places. But he was spotted.

The rifleman was looking in the other direction, and when he saw Pettigrew coming he had to turn half-around to take aim. Pettigrew's eyes caught that little movement, and he dropped off the right side of his horse at the same time the rifle cracked.

Rowdy wasn't used to being dismounted from the off side, and he snorted and jumped. The rifle slug plowed a furrow across the seat of the saddle. Pettigrew kept hold of the reins and kept the horse between him and the shooter. The rifle cracked again. Rowdy dropped to his knees, then fell over with a bullet in the heart.

Pettigrew screamed, "You son of a bitch. You God damn son of a bitch." Then he knew he was a fool for standing there yelling, and he fell to the ground behind the dying horse. Rowdy's hind legs twitched. His lungs pumped for a few more seconds. Then he was still.

Muttering, cursing, Pettigrew looked over the horse's body for the shooter. "You God damne mean bloodthirsty son of a bitch. You didn't have to shoot this horse. Show yourself, God damn you."

The bell mare had trotted away a short distance, carrying a bedroll, a skillet, a coffee pot and a few groceries, all tied down with a lash cinch. She stopped when she stepped on the lead rope. Pettigrew wished she would run, get safely away, but she stood watching him, ears twitching. He yelled, "Run, you fool. Get away."

The rifle cracked a third time. But instead of seeking the horse, the angry slug zipped past Pettigrew's head, forcing him down. He cursed and muttered.

Knowing he was too far for an accurate pistol shot, Pettigrew raised his head, aimed the Colt a little high and fired five shots, hoping for luck. When the hammer clicked on an empty, he ducked and hastily reloaded. Three rapid shots came from the rifleman, two of them hitting the dead horse and the third burning away into space. Pettigrew took six more cartridges from his belt, held them in his right hand for a fast reload, then fired the Colt again until it clicked. It was a searching fire. Pettigrew could only hope that at least one slug would come down where it would do some damage. No such luck.

Four shots came from the rifleman. But Pettigrew was flat behind the dead horse, reloading. After filling the six chambers, he had three cartridges left. So far, his searching shots had missed the target, but he believed the more shots he fired the better his chances.

He was safe behind the dead horse. The rifleman couldn't hit him here. But he didn't intend to stay here the rest of the day, either. He stayed down a minute, thinking.

He'd killed four men in the past few weeks. He'd

never wanted to kill anyone—until now. Now he wanted to kill. He muttered, "You dirty sorry rotten yellow belly bastard. You ain't fit to live. No, by god, you ain't fit to live."

So he'd have only three rounds left. Well, by god, he wasn't going to just lie there. Pettigrew raised his head and gun hand again, and again fired six shots, scattering the shots, covering as much of the ground over there as he could.

Shoving in the remaining three bullets, he expected answering fire, but none came. He waited, knowing he had to conserve ammunition now. Did that bastard over there know he had only three shots left? He knew by now that Pettigrew had no rifle. Could he use that to his advantage some way?

Maybe Pettigrew would have to wait until dark to get away. Maybe Beans was somewhere near and would hear the gunfire. Maybe Beans was dead, killed by that sorry piece of hogshit over there. Or—and now Pettigrew had something else to worry about—maybe that low-life would come out of the weeds and circle behind him. That scum didn't have to worry about being in the open as long as he stayed out of pistol range. Pettigrew had to keep watch behind him now. If he saw the man, he'd have to change positions right fast, get on the other side of the dead horse.

Uh-oh. Something was happening over there. There was movement. Suddenly a man on a horse rode out from the trees, spurring hard. He'd had a horse tied over there somewhere. He was going to get behind Pettigrew. Pettigrew got ready to move fast.

But no. The rider carried no rifle. He was bent over the horse's neck, hanging onto the saddle horn with both hands. He was hurt.

"God damn," Pettigrew said, standing. He had a

strong urge to go after him. How? It would take terrific strength to pull his saddle from under the dead horse. Without Rowdy, he'd have to yank the load off the bell mare and ride her bareback. The bushwhacker was leaving on a hard run. Pettigrew couldn't catch him.

He cursed again. He'd give half of what he owned to catch and kill that man. Pettigrew didn't know his name, but he knew what he looked like. He was the one who'd had the shotgun over by Hardscrabble. And he'd tried to kill Pettigrew one, two, three, four times now. He'd killed Pettigrew's favorite horse just out of damned meanness. If there was a chance in the world of catching him, Pettigrew would go after him.

Come to think of it . . .

Pettigrew smiled a wicked smile. The man was hit, no doubt about that. One of the searching shots had found him, and he had a .45 slug in him. He was headed for Canon City, and he'd either fall out of the saddle and die before he got there or he'd hunt up the doctor. If the doctor saved him, Pettigrew would kill him.

Believing the danger was over for now, Pettigrew walked and led the bell mare, getting his boots wet. There was no horse in the corral, no smoke from the cabin chimney. Beans wasn't there. He unloaded the horse, put her in the corral and carried his bed and gear inside. Beans' bed was rolled up and stashed against a wall in the bedroom. He was planning to be back.

Dark was coming fast, and Pettigrew wanted to get his saddle from under the dead horse and get to town. To the bell mare, he said, "You'll stand for just about anything, old girl. Now let me put some harness on you." She fidgeted some when he buckled a collar around her neck and threw the harness on,

151

but allowed him to do it. With a singletree hitched to the near tug, he led the horse across the creek, getting his boots wet again, and hitched the single-tree to the saddle horn. He clucked and slapped the mare on the rump with the driving lines. She pulled the saddle free.

"I wish I could say your day's work is done, old girl, but I've got to get to town and its too close to dark to find the other horses." He put the saddle on her back without cinching it down and let her carry it and the harness back to the corral. There he stripped the harness off and cinched the saddle on. He mounted and said, "Let's go to town."

The sheriff's office was dark, locked. Pettigrew stopped a well-dressed man and asked if he knew where the U.S. marshal was. No, the man said, but the marshal was somewhere in town. On horseback again, Pettigrew rode to the doctor's combination home and clinic. He tied the mare to a hitchrail, walked up a short stone path, stepped up onto a wide porch and knocked on the door. The man who opened the door wasn't the doctor. It was the hard-faced, slit-eyed U.S. Marshal Dodds. A grimace that was meant to be a wry smile creased the marshal's face.

He said, "Well, look who's here. You just saved me a ride." He came out onto the porch, and a gun appeared in his right hand. Just appeared. "Reach for the rafters, mister. You're under arrest."

Pettigrew's shoulders slumped. He sighed. "What now?"

"I knew I'd get the goods on you sooner or later. Reach, I said." The gun was aimed at Pettigrew's heart. The marshal was a professional gunman. Pettigrew sighed again and slowly raised his hands. His

Colt was yanked from its holster. The marshal backed up a few steps, the grimace still on his face. "Yessir, I knew I'd get you for something."

"All right," Pettigrew said with resignation, "what is it you got me for?"

"Murder. Pure and simple."

"Whose murder?"

"That man in there on the doctor's table. He just died."

"Aw, for—"

"He lived long enough to tell me what happened. You shot him. All he wanted was to buy a few cows from you and you shot him."

"That's a lie."

"Nope. A dyin' man don't lie."

"If that's what he told you then he's a damned liar. He shot at me from ambush. He shot my horse. I shot back."

"Seems to me you told that story before. You got by with it once. By god, you won't get by with it again."

It was a long night. He lay on the iron bunk in the jail and worried. The damned marshal hadn't even tried to find out the dead man's name. If Pettigrew was going to be charged with murder they had to know the victim's name. Didn't they? And if they found out his name they could find out what kind of man he was. Would that make any difference? It ought to, but would it? It was Pettigrew's word against the word of a dying man. The prosecuting attorney couldn't produce one witness. But then, neither could Pettigrew.

The most damaging evidence against him was another dead man—Muley Reece. Muley had been killed in almost exactly the same way. Pettigrew's story had been believed once. It would not be believed again.

There would be a trial. A good lawyer could help, but he had no money for lawyer fees.

Then another thought popped into Pettigrew's mind: he'd killed five men now. It would be hard to convince a jury that it was all in self-defense.

Pettigrew lay on his back with his arm over his eyes, muttering, "Hell's hooks."

He was served a breakfast of hotcakes with no syrup or meat. The coffee was lukewarm. A runt of a man from the Canyon Cafe brought it over, and the marshal watched with a gun in his hand when the tin plate and cup was slid under the cell door.

Pettigrew asked, "Did you take care of my horse?"

"What horse?" the marshal said.

"God damn, do you mean you left that horse standing tied to a hitchrail all night?"

"Don't go badmouthing me, mister. You think you got troubles? I can give you a hell of a lot more."

"I'm entitled to bail."

"Only the judge can set bail, and he ain't here."

"Well, get him."

"He ain't due here 'til day after tomorrow. You'll just have to wait. Besides, you ain't got no money for bail anyhow."

"I'm a property owner. I can put up some property."

"That's for the judge to decide."

"All right." Pettigrew fixed the runt with his gaze. "I want you to be a witness. If that mare ain't taken somewhere and fed and watered, the damned state or county or somdamnbody is gonna pay."

"Don't worry, mister," the runt said. "I hear things over to the cafe, and I heard that the doctor saw your horse standin' out there this mornin' and got somebody to take care of her."

Still angry, still bitter, Pettigrew said, "Just remember, and spread the word, it was the doctor that

154

did it and not this so-called lawman."

Casting a glance at the marshal, the runt left. The hard-eyed marshal stayed a moment, scowling at his prisoner, then turned on his heel and stomped through the connecting door.

District Judge George Walls was a no-nonsense man. He demanded that everyone stand when he strode into the courtroom wearing his black robe. "Be seated," he said after he'd stepped up onto a small platform and taken a seat behind a big oak desk. Only a handful of townsmen were in the half-finished courtroom on the second floor of Fremont County's half-finished stone courthouse. They were attracted by Pettigrew being marched to the court-house in handcuffs, the marshal walking behind with a gun in his hand. Also present was an officious-looking young man in a dark Prince Albert coat, white shirt with a stiff collar and a wide necktie.

All construction work had stopped while the court was in session.

No one spoke as the judge shuffled papers on the desk. Then he looked down from his perch at the humble citizens. "Now then, we have here the matter of Lemual Pettigrew versus the state of Colorado. Mr. Prosecutor, have formal charges been filed?"

"That is why we are here, Your Honor. The district attorney's office is charging Lemual Pettigrew with murder in the second degree. We believe the murder was not premeditated, but was the result of an argument over the sale of some cattle."

"Have you identified the deceased?"

The young man shot his cuffs and ran his hands down the length of his coat, trying to smooth travel wrinkles. "No, Your Honor. The deceased carried no identification."

Pettigrew interrupted, "Nobody tried to identify him."

Bang went the judge's gavel. "Mr. Pettigrew, this is not a trial. You will be given your opportunity to be heard when the time comes. Now then, you are being charged with second degree murder. How do you plead?"

"Not guilty."

"Very well. Now then, we have the matter of bond. Does the prosecutor have a recommendation?"

"Your Honor, the district attorney's office recommends that no bail be set."

"Mr. Pettigrew, what do you say?"

"Sir, I own a half section of land five miles east of town. I have a two-room house and other improvements. I also own eighty-five head of cattle and four horses. No bond should be necessary."

"Very well. The charge of second degree murder is bondable. I am going to set bond at two thousand dollars. Mr. Pettigrew, you may arrange with the county clerk to place a lien on your property for that amount or you may post cash bond. Mr. Prosecutor, when will you be ready to go to trial?"

"Why, uh, soon, Your Honor. Say, uh, September fifteen."

"Is that suitable for you, Mr. Pettigrew?"

Pettigrew shrugged. "As far as I know now."

"Very well, trial is set for September fifteen. Now then, I see nothing more on the docket. This court is adjourned." Judge Walls stood and abruptly left the room.

"Let's go see the county clerk," Pettigrew said, "and get this over with."

The marshal's face was as hard as ever. "We'll go see the county clerk when I say we will."

There seemed to be nothing Pettigrew could do about it so he said nothing. Again he was marched down the street wearing handcuffs while the towns-people stared. Back in his cell, Pettigrew sat on the iron cot with his head in his hands. He was entitled to bail, but the damned marshal was going to make him wait to post it. He needed somebody on the outside to help him. Beans was gone somewhere, and Betsy . . . Betsy hadn't even come to see him. There was no one else.

Pettigrew's stomach was growling from hunger when the slit-eyed marshal unlocked the cell door and swung it open. "You're bonded out. Get out. But don't even think of leaving the county." Puzzled, Pettigrew walked uncertainly out of the jail and through the connecting door. He stopped suddenly and stared, not believing what he was seeing.

Cynthia Atkinson said, "At last, Mr. Pettigrew, I can begin to repay my debt to you."

Chapter Twenty-one

He was handed his wallet and gunbelt. It only took a second to count the money in his wallet. There wasn't much. His horse, he was told, was in a barn on the south end of town, and he'd have to pay for its keep.

Outside, on the boardwalk, Mrs. Atkinson took his arm and said, "We need to talk."

"Yeah, that we do."

She had her hair combed down to her shoulders, bunched around her face, and tied with a white ribbon. Her dress showed class — good covert cloth, dark blue with ruffles on all the edges. It came down to her soft leather button-up shoes. "Is there any place were we can talk privately?"

"None that I know of. My homestead is five miles from here. You don't want to go there."

"No. I, — I just arrived on the stage about an hour ago, and I'm planning to go back to Pueblo tonight. Is there a decent restaurant here?"

"There's the Royal. We can sit at a table and have a little privacy."

"That will have to do, then."

The owner of the Royal Restaurant, the Home of Fine Dining, had tried for elegance by putting clean linen cloths on the tables and having the menus printed in an Old English scroll. The floor was uncovered but clean, and the waitresses wore long clean aprons. It was the tables and chairs that failed to fit the decor. They were made by a local craftsman of pinewood, unpolished and rustic.

Pettigrew knew he was out of place here. He'd shaved in cold water the day before, but he'd slept in his clothes for six days, his eyes were hollow and his face was haggard. The few patrons stared at the beautiful lady being escorted by a saddle tramp. They strained their ears when the couple occupied a table in a far corner, leaned close to each other and talked in low tones, at times whispering.

"I wish we had more privacy," Mrs. Atkinson said, "but this will have to do, for the time being anyway. I have a proposition for you."

Pettigrew said nothing, just waited for her to go on.

"Let me explain. As I told you, I have no legal claim to Charles' estate, but I engaged an attorney in Chicago to see if I could salvage something from it. He thought that if we went before a jury the jury might award me something, but not much. Jurors, it seems, have little use for women who take up residence with another woman's husband." She paused to see if Pettigrew understood. He nodded.

"But my attorney—"

She was interrupted by a waitress who had a pad of paper and a pencil in her hand. Mrs. Atkinson ordered only coffee. Pettigrew was hungry, but remembering how little money he had, he ordered only toast.

The lady had her arms folded on top of the table. She leaned closer. "As I was about to say, my attorney is shrewd. He took advantage of the slow-turning wheels of justice by threatening her attorney with a long delay in getting the matter settled. He could have done it, too. He convinced her attorney that he had enough of a case to keep the estate tied up in court for a year or more."

Pettigrew nodded again.

"Her attorney would have liked that. The longer the matter dragged on the bigger his fee would be. But she didn't like it."

A cut-glass pitcher of water and two glasses were placed on the table. Pettigrew poured water in the lady's glass, then filled his own. Both drank deeply. Mrs. Atkinson talked on:

"She's greedy. She wants to go abroad. She wants as much money as she can get as quickly as she can get it. So the two attorneys settled out of court. I got ten thousand dollars after attorney's fees. That will keep me for two years or longer, depending on how I live. I mean, it would have. I just paid two thousand dollars to get you out of jail."

Pettigrew started to apologize, but she waved one hand, and added, "Don't worry about that. I owe it to you. Also, if you show up in court at the appointed time I get the money back. But . . ."

Her coffee and his toast were placed on the table in china dishes. His plate had a chip on one side, but he couldn't have cared less. The toast went untouched for the moment.

"What I started to say, Mr. Pettigrew — may I call you Lemual?"

"Lem."

"Lem, then. Please call me Cynthia. What I started to say is someone is being dishonest. Do you remember the fifty thousand dollars ransom? Of course you do. Well, guess what? It wasn't included in the inventory of Charles' assets." She stopped talking, took a sip of her coffee and leaned back in her chair. "What do you think?"

With a half-grin, he shook his head. "Like you said, somebody is being dishonest."

Leaning forward again, she said, "I did not mention it to the Chicago attorneys. As far as everyone in Chicago is concerned, that money doesn't exist. I intend to find it and recover it.

160

And that, Lem, is where I need your help."

"How can I help? I'm no lawyer."

"A lawyer is the last kind of man I need. Mr. Pettigrew — Lem, you have been a detective. Where would you start looking?"

He mulled it over a moment. "I have to think about it. We have to talk some more. But not here. Did you say you're staying in Pueblo?"

"Yes. At the same hotel."

It was something to think about, all right. Fifty thousand dollars was missing. He might be able to find it, but this woman had been bad news from the first time he'd heard of her. So she'd just put up two thousand dollars to get him out of jail. She owed him her life. Don't go following her without knowing what you're doing, Lem Pettigrew, he told himself. To her he said "Maybe I can ride over there in a few days. Right now I've got to get home. I've been gone too much this summer, and I've got work to do."

"Of course. But please come to see me soon. I don't know what happened to that money, but I have a hunch that the quicker we start looking for it the easier it will be to find."

"You're probably right. I'll get over there in a few days."

"Is that a promise?"

"Unless I break a leg or get shot, that's a promise."

At home, Pettigrew located his horses, corralled them, cut out a dun gelding and turned the others free again, the bell mare with them. Inside the cabin he discovered that every bite of meat he had was spoiled. He fixed a meatless supper and decided he'd have to go hunting before he did anything else. That reminded him he had no rifle, and that reminded him that the would-be killer had shot at him with a rifle, but was hanging onto his saddle with both hands when he rode away. Pettigrew searched the weeds along the creek and just before dark found a lever action carbine.

In the cabin, by lamplight, he jerked the lever down repeatedly until the gun kicked out one empty cartridge and three live ones. There were no more. They were the blunt .44-.40s.

Riding the high country next day, Pettigrew realized that living off the fat of the land was a very uncertain way of living. He saw no sign of deer, but at midafternoon he shot a turkey. He was back home plucking feathers when he saw Beans Gipson coming.

Beans hollered, "Hallo-o," before he rode across the creek into the yard. "You're just in time for supper," Pettigrew said, still working on the bird. "Been somewhere?"

Dismounting, squatting on his heels, Beans said, "Been to Canon City, been to Pueblo, been back to Canon City. Got there last night. I heard about your latest adventures." He grinned. "Partner, you just cain't stay out of trouble."

A wry grin touched Pettigrew's face. "I started something that won't end."

"That makes five dead men now, don't it?"

"Five."

"Well," Beans drawled, "I found out who the last 'un is—was."

At that, Pettigrew stopped plucking feathers and looked up. "You did? Who was he?"

"Name was Milstone or Millston or somethin' like that. Had a beer in the O.K. Saloon, and met a feller that knew somethin' about 'im. Said there was two brothers that done nothin' but hang around the saloon, drink and play cards. Said they disappeared for a while, 'bout the same time that kid deputy did, then a few days ago one of 'em showed up. Said him and another man took a look at the corpse before they buried it."

162

"Brothers, huh? That could explain it."

"It could."

"That might help at my trial."

"It might. But I learned somethin' else when I was in the pen. I learned you cain't second-guess a jury. A feller in there swears he's innocent, but a jury found 'im guilty anyways."

"Huh," Pettigrew snorted. "That's good to know."

They cut some hay along Cripple Creek north of the homesteads where the grass grew high. With only one scythe, they took turns cutting. They nailed some tall sticks to the sides of the light wagon, which enabled them to stack hay in it. Beans rode a horse instead of riding in the wagon, and he always took his saddle bags with him. For four days they cut and hauled hay. At the end of the fourth day Pettigrew got a shot at a young buck, and they had fresh meat again. Pettigrew allowed he had enough hay to feed two horses through the coming winter. He'd cut some more off a small meadow farther north. But first he had some business to take care of.

"You're a good butcher, Beans. Cut me a couple of good steaks, will you?"

"You goin' callin'?"

"Yep, but I ain't calling on a woman. Ever hear of a town called Hardscrabble?"

"Naw."

"It's got a population of one. I owe that gent. The least I can do is take him some fresh meat and say thanks again."

"Before you go, partner, there's somethin' I'd like for you to think about."

"What?" Pettigrew put some dish water on the stove to heat.

Beans tilted his chair back on its hind legs. "Sellin' this outfit."

"Huh?" Pettigrew stopped what he was doing. "What're you talking about?"

"Sellin' it. How much would you take for it?"

"Hell, I don't know. Who wants to buy it?"

"Me."

For a moment, Pettigrew didn't know what to say. Then, "Aw, come on, Beans. What're you talking about? Where would you get the money?"

"I've got it. Name a price."

"What did you do, rob a bank?"

"Didn't have to." He let his chair down, put his elbows on the table. "One of the fellers I got acquainted with in the pen is a gambler. I mean, he made his livin' playin' cards. He don't cheat. He don't have to. He knows the odds. He's got it stashed in his head. A pal of his outside bribed a guard to fetch him five decks of cards, and me and him played with them cards six, eight, ten hours a day. We wore 'em out. I learned how to play poker."

This, Pettigrew surmised, was going to be a long story. He sat across the table and listened.

"There's two tricks to winnin' at poker. First one is knowin' the odds, knowin' when to raise and when to fold. You won't win ever' hand that way, but you'll win more'n you'll lose. The second one is to stay awake. Some of the big poker games go on all night and all day and all the next night. The gent that stays awake and keeps thinkin' is gonna win. Me and him played cards for two days and nights at a time just for practice. And, oh yeah, don't let nobody cheat. He learned me ever' cheatin' trick there is. I know when somebody is tryin' to cheat."

Pettigrew said, "Are you gonna tell me you got rich playing cards?"

"Let me show you somethin'." Beans went to the bedroom and returned carrying his saddle bags. He opened one, took out a bundle wrapped in muslin and unwrapped it. It was a bundle of greenbacks. "Now, what'll you take for this outfit?"

"Well, for . . ." All Pettigrew could do was shake his head.

"I started at Canon City, won a little, went to Pueblo, won some more, then got in a big game with some boys that had money to burn. We played for two days, only stoppin' long enough to go outside and pee. I won. That's all there is to it."

"Huh." That was all Pettigrew could say.

" 'Nother thing my pal in the pen learned me. He said first time winners think it's easy. They think all they have to do is play cards and live like a king. No matter how good you are you cain't always win. Said when he gets out he ain't gonna play cards. He's got him a stash, and he's goin' into business. His pa was in the mercantile business, and that's what he's gonna do. I been thinkin' ever since I come back here, all the time we was cuttin' hay. I got a good stake here, but I c'd lose it as fast as I won it. I'm through playin' cards."

Astonishment was plain on Pettigrew's face. "You . . . you don't mean it?"

"I mean it, partner. Whatta ya say?"

"Well . . . well, I don't know offhand."

"Think about it, will yu?"

"Yeah. Yeah, I'll think about it."

Chapter Twenty-two

Pettigrew thought about it. While he rode southeast, down the front range of the Sierra Mojadas, he thought about it. He'd been worried about the coming winter. He wondered if Beans had enough money to buy groceries for himself and hay for his horses. Cattle could forage for themselves—unless the winter was unusually harsh. But horses, if they were working, had to be fed in the winter. And harsh winters happened. A cattleman had to be prepared.

If I was smart, Pettigrew said to himself, I'd get out while I can. But no. He'd worked too hard for that ranch. It was the first time in his life he'd owned more than a horse, a saddle and a bedroll.

He turned uphill and came to the place where he'd rescued the woman, where a sheriff and Mr. Atkinson were killed. Looking around for his rifle, he guessed that the killers had taken it. When he found some empty bottle-neck cartridge cases, he knew his rifle had been used in the ambush of the two.

Riding on uphill he came to the draw where he'd caught part of a load of buckshot, and the scrub cedars he'd tried to hide in. The memory caused him to shake his head in sorrow. Seven men killed. One a sheriff and the other a rich Easterner, and still it wasn't over.

What was left of the settlement called Hardscrabble was exactly the way he'd seen it last, except that no smoke was coming from the stone chimney of the one occupied shack. It took Pettigrew a few seconds to figure out what was different. The burro was there, but the burro wasn't tied to anything, nor hobbled.

It saw Pettigrew and his horse, and brayed. It started walking toward them. "Gets lonesome being the only equine around, doesn't it, feller," Pettigrew said. "Where's your master?" The burro followed them when he rode on.

"Hallo-o," he yelled at the cabin door. A cold fear went through him. Something was wrong. He dismounted, dropped the reins and opened the door, half-expecting to find the nameless man dead.

But he didn't. He searched the room, even looked under the bed. Everything was clean. The dishes had been washed and put away. Except for one coffee cup that sat in the middle of the table on top of a sheet of white paper. A message had been written on the paper. Pettigrew picked it up, carried it closer to the door where the light was better and read:

Do not look for my body. You will never find it. I died by my own hand. It was my life and I can end it if I want to. What few dollars I have should go to the charity ward of the nearest hospital. My books and my target rifle are the only things I have of value. Sell them and turn the proceeds over to the hospital. Goodbye.

The note was not signed.

Pettigrew groaned. "Oh no . . ." He sat on the door step a moment, then stood and walked around the cabin, to the creek and back. He wasn't looking for anything in particular — just anything. "Damn,

167

damn, damn," he muttered. The nameless man was right, there were a thousand places in the mountains where he could lie down and die and never be found. But his rifle was hanging from spikes on the far wall, so how did he die? He was a doctor. He knew all about poisons and injections and things like that. Which did he choose? And why did he choose to die?

Pettigrew opened the wooden box at the end of the room. The black medical bag wasn't there. In a leather purse he found fifteen dollars and some silver change, a heavy mackinaw and a few other articles of clothing. Nothing more. The doctor was a mystery in life and in death. Outside, Pettigrew sat on the ground and tried to remember everything the doctor had said. Stay away from trouble. Stay away from crowds. "Huh," Pettigrew said aloud, ". . . stay away from everything."

What else? Stay away from women. The male urges are terrible. Yeah, that's what he'd said. The sins of the flesh. What did he say about that? Destructive. Destroyed many a man.

Did the doctor bed the wrong woman? He'd done something disgraceful, something he thought was disgraceful. It got him kicked out of his profession. He couldn't face the world and tried to hide from it. Whatever he'd done it had to do with a woman. Or maybe a young girl.

Maybe Sheriff Bowen at Pueblo could find out. Maybe not. Pettigrew had to report it to the sheriff. That brought a groan from him. More questions from a lawman. More explaining. "Well," he said aloud as he shut the cabin door, ". . . it has to be reported."

It was late at night when Pettigrew rode into Pueblo. He was tired and his horse was tired. The cost for feeding the horse that night and again in the morning was thirty cents, he was told. He paid, then walked, carrying his saddle bags, to the sheriff's office. Nope, said a tall, lanky deputy with a hogleg pistol on his right hip, the sheriff was t'home. But when he heard what Pettigrew had found at Hardscrabble, he said, "Wait right here," and went to fetch his boss.

Sheriff Bowen knew about Pettigrew's background and wasn't as suspicious as the U.S. Marshal at Canon City, but he had to hear the complete story about everything that had happened at Hardscrabble, in the Mojadas and in Rosita.

Leaning back in his swivel chair in the bottom floor of the Pueblo County courthouse, the sheriff fingered his handlebar moustache and said, "Did you touch anything in the cabin?"

Pettigrew considered telling the truth, but changed his mind. Why invite more questions? "No, but I couldn't ignore the note." He told the sheriff everything he could remember about his conversation with the nameless doctor.

"Sure is a mystery," the sheriff mused, still fingering his moustache. "Well, we'll have to ride out there in the morning and see what we can see. If we could just find out where he come from . . . we've got a telegraph here."

"A telegraph," Pettigrew allowed, "can sometimes be a lawman's best friend."

He couldn't afford a hotel room, so he went to a flop house, paid fifteen cents for a cot and a place to wash. He looked over the big room full of sleeping, snoring, tossing men, then flopped down on his rented army surplus cot and slept with his hat over his face. In the morning he had to wait his turn at the one wash basin, but when he left the Arkansaw Hotel he was freshly shaved.

She was sitting at a table for four in the Pueblo

Hotel's dining room, sipping coffee. The china plate before her held the remains of toast and marmalade. He wondered as he walked in whether she missed her morning rides and having breakfast served in her room. If she did, she didn't show it.

"Oh, am I glad to see you," she exclaimed. "I was beginning to think you weren't coming." She was easily one of the most beautiful women he'd ever seen. Now her red hair was swept up and tied with a green ribbon on top of her head. She wore a silver chain necklace hung with an emerald and matching earrings.

"I apologize," he said, aware of his wrinkled, rancher's clothes. "I just had to get some work done." He accepted her invitation to sit, and yes, he would like a cup of coffee. In fact, he hungrily eyed the remains of her toast, but he tried not to let it show. That reminded him of two good buckskin steaks he had in his saddle bags. For lunch he'd broil them over an open fire out on the desert somewhere, if they hadn't spoiled.

"I trust this is more than just a social visit," she said, and added, "Not that I wouldn't welcome a social visit. Seems everyone here has learned that Mr. Atkinson and I were not legally married, and a body would think I had the measles."

Chuckling, Pettigrew said, "No—I've been thinking about your proposition. As I recall, though, we didn't mention my share of any money I might recover."

"Forty-sixty. How's that?"

"Fifty-fifty."

She smiled. Her teeth were like perfect pearls. "You deserve it, Lem. Have you any idea where to start?"

After glancing around, he said, "I've been up to your room before. Can we go up there again? There

170

are too many ears in here."

"Of course. The desk clerk might not like it, but, if you'll pardon my language, to hell with him."

He followed her up the curving stairs, admiring her backside. Which reminded him he hadn't had a woman for . . . too damned long. This room wasn't as big, and had no private water closet. There was no table to sit at either, but there were two chairs. They sat facing each other, Pettigrew with his hat in his lap.

"Now then, Lem, what do you think?"

He was quiet a moment, trying to think of a tactful way to ask the question he had in mind. Finally, he worked his way through it. "Mrs. Atkinson, there's, uh, there's something that's been bothering me. I apologize in advance if I'm wrong, but . . ."

"It's Cynthia, remember, and you're right."

"I'm right?"

"Yes. I knew that when you started thinking about it you'd come to the proper conclusion."

"Well, there was some clues. Muley Reece said something like, 'Don't worry about her.' And another man lying on his belly with my gun aimed at him, he said something like that too. And a gunshot—a shot you fired—that warned away the men with the money."

She smiled a quick smile. "However, the second kidnapping was definitely not my idea. You really did save my life then."

All he could do was stare at the carpeted floor and nod.

"I owe you an explanation." She took a deep breath. "What I'm about to tell you is strictly between you and me. Agreed? Can I trust you?"

"Uh-huh. I mean, yes, unless you're going to tell me about a crime or something."

"I have done nothing illegal."

171

"All right."

"I'll be blunt. Mr. Charles B. Atkinson was a brute. That's putting it mildly. He was a bastard. He was an obnoxious, perverted son of a bitch. Pardon my language, but I can't think of a more appropriate description."

Surprise showed on Pettigrew's face.

"Like everyone else, you wouldn't have thought it. That, Lem, is because you've never lived with him. Slept with him." A pause, then, "Oh, yes, there is another adjective that fits. He was rich."

"Uh-huh."

A bitter frown turned down the corners of her mouth. "He was so damnably charming in public. At home, in a bedroom, he . . . well, now you can guess the rest of the story."

"Yeah," he said.

"I spent nearly a year with that man, pretending to be his loving wife, thinking that eventually I would be his wife. I was as loyal as a wife could be, and it never even occurred to me to be unfaithful. But gradually I began to realize that I didn't want to be his wife. I didn't want to live with him. I wanted out. But — can you understand this, Lem — I had a year invested in him, and I thought I was entitled to something."

He only nodded.

"If Charles had known how I felt he would have . . . I don't know what he would have done. He loved me, I'm sure of that. He would have given me anything as long as I was living with him. But if I walked out he would have given me nothing. I was desperate. Can you understand?"

Silence. Then he said, "How you met him and all that, I can guess."

"I have a higher education. I was brought up in a good family. I socialized with the right people." A

172

flush stole up her cheeks.

Lem nodded again.

"But what I can't guess is how you got acquainted with the three so-called kidnappers."

Another quick smile. "It was by accident. I was walking on the sidewalks one evening when a drunk bumped me. Homer—he was the one who went after the money—saw what happened and chastised the drunk, then offered to walk me to my hotel. Homer was obviously a laborer, but he was a gentleman. Two days later I met him again as I was riding my mare back from the end of the railroad. He was also riding to town. We talked. I had already concocted the scheme, and I just bluntly asked him if he would like to earn an easy couple of thousand dollars. He got Jackson, a friend of his, to assist, and the scheme was carried out. The other one, Muley Reece, was recruited to lead the sheriff and his deputies away from us. I—none of us knew he was homicidal. We had no intention of harming anyone. We all told him not to shoot you out there in the Royal Gorge, only to keep you there until dark."

"How did you know you could trust them? Why would they settle for a couple thousand dollars apiece while you took forty-six thousand?"

"I was prepared." She stood, opened a bureau drawer and showed him a pearl-handled, silver-plated revolver. "This was hidden in my clothes."

"I heard you're a target shooter, but could you shoot a man?"

"If he was threatening me physically, yes. Only then. If I were the type, I could have shot you up there. You weren't watching me."

"Hmm. You could have, all right. Well, if it hadn't been for me your scheme would have worked."

"You didn't spoil our plan. If you'll remember, Homer and Jackson got away from you with the

173

money."

Pettigrew had to grin. "With your help. You sure had me fooled."

"It was the crooked murderous deputy and his cohorts who killed Homer and Jackson, then Charles and the sheriff from Canon City."

They fell silent again. Homer and Jackson. Pettigrew hadn't counted them. That made nine dead men. All because of a scheme this woman had cooked up. But was it her fault? After all, five of the nine were killers themselves. Now she had another scheme, and she wanted his help. He knew what it was.

And he knew that it too could end in gunfire.

Chapter Twenty-Three

The woman known as Mrs. Charles Atkinson sat quietly, her hands in her lap, fingers twitching nervously. "Now you know more about me than anyone else in the world."

Grinning a wry grin, Pettigrew said, "It's an interesting story. In fact, if you'll pardon my language, it's the damnedest story I ever heard."

"Do you believe me?"

"I don't claim to know so much about people that I can't be fooled, but yes, I believe you."

"Do you want to earn half of fifty thousand dollars?"

"I do."

"Where do we start?"

Pettigrew studied his dirty grey hat, turning it over in his hands. It was a good Stetson he'd bought when he had more money, and it was in good shape, though sweat-stained. "Like you said, somebody is being dishonest, and it's either the sheriff or the lawyer. Probably the lawyer. The sheriff couldn't get by with it." He looked up. "Do you remember the name of the lawyer?"

"Clawson. I believe his first name is Everett."

"You said he showed you a court order. Did you read it — every word?"

She was hesitant. "Well, I . . . I must admit, Lem, I was very upset about the whole matter, and it was a long list of Charles' assets in Colorado, and I'm definitely not a business person. Perhaps I didn't read it carefully."

"I don't understand all I know about this legal stuff, but surely he had to have a court order of some kind."

"Oh yes, he showed me a signature of a judge. It was written in a flourishing style, and I didn't try to read it. But the print under it said he was a district court judge. There was also a raised seal."

Standing, Pettigrew said. "The first man to see is the sheriff. See what became of the money." Then he snapped his fingers and said, "Oh, I almost forgot. The sheriff is out of town. He had to go to Hardscrabble. You remember Hardscrabble, the ghost town where your kidnappers, the second bunch, tried to shoot us out of a cabin? Well, the man that helped me drive them off is — was — a little strange. I went to pay him a visit yesterday, and he wasn't there. I think he killed himself."

"Oh, my." She put a hand to her throat.

"Anyway, that's where the sheriff is supposed to be today."

"Then, do you think we should visit the lawyer?"

"I guess so. I'd rather hear what the sheriff has to say first, but I don't want to wait."

"Should I go with you?"

"It might help. When he sees you he'll know what we're talking about."

He waited in the hotel lobby while she powdered her nose and did whatever else a lady had to do before going out on the street. When she came down the stairs, holding her skirts above her buttoned shoes with one hand, he was again made to realize that she was a beautiful lady while he looked like a saddle tramp.

The office of Everett Clawson was easy to find. It was a one-story frame building two doors from Pueblo's new three-story courthouse. A sign on a post in front read: EVERETT CLAWSON: ATTORNEY AT LAW.

But the attorney at law wasn't in. A pretty young woman sitting at a receptionist's desk informed them that Mr. Clawson was in Denver and wasn't expected back for two days. They started to leave, then Pettigrew turned back. "Does he go to Denver very often?"

"Now and then, yes."

Pettigrew was worried. He walked alongside Mrs. Atkinson quietly for a half block, boots thumping on the plank walk, then said, "He probably put the money in a bank in Denver."

She stopped and faced him. "That will make it more difficult to recover, won't it?"

"Yeah, but . . . well, we couldn't expect him to carry it around in his pockets." They walked on, Pettigrew deep in thought. Finally, he said, "It's not hopeless, but we can't do a thing until he gets back. Then we'll have to try first one thing and then another."

"Should we call on the judge?"

"No, not yet. It's possible that no judge signed that order. The whole thing could have been forged. Or maybe the judge signed the order but didn't check the list of assets. Either way we don't want any judge to know about the missing money."

"You are absolutely right."

"Well." Pettigrew's thoughts then turned to his other problems. He'd had no breakfast and he didn't have the price of a meal. Asking her for living expenses while they waited was out of the question. He'd have to go home. At home he had groceries, if nothing else. And he'd have to sell a calf or a horse or something to raise some cash. "Mrs. uh, Cynthia, I have to go home to attend to some business. I'll be back in two or three days."

"I wish you didn't have to go."

"I do too. I'll be back, and that's a promise."

He was no more than a mile out of town when he dismounted in a sandy draw, built a fire of sagebrush and broiled the two steaks he'd been carrying in his saddlebags. He ate both of them, and wished for another.

It was well after dark when he rode up to his cabin. A dim lamp light in the window and a horse in the corral told him Beans was there. Just the same he yelled "Hallo" and waited for Beans to open the door before he got down.

"I just got back myself," Beans said. "Been over to Canon City. You et?"

"Not since about noon."

"I roasted some buckskin ribs and had 'em for supper last night. There's some left over. I can heat 'em up."

"I'll eat anything," Pettigrew grinned. "Even some of your beans."

In the morning the sky was overcast, promising rain. "It's good and bad," Pettigrew allowed. "We need the rain, but I can't harvest hay when it's wet."

"Nope. You stack wet hay and all you'll have is a pile of stinkin' mold."

"Anyway, I've got to find a way to make some money. Sell a calf, I guess. I'm busted."

"I'm still ready and willin' to buy your whole durned outfit."

"It ain't for sale. I'd sell you a horse but you don't need another one."

"This outfit needs all the horses you've got."

"Yeah, but . . ." Pettigrew stepped to the door and looked at the sky again. "I guess I'll go talk to Clyde Hanson that owns the butcher shop in Canon City, see if he wants a live calf or if he wants to butcher it here."

Clyde Hanson wasn't in either. He'd gone to a ranch west of town to look at some beeves, Pettigrew was told.

"Aw, dammit," he said outside. "Nobody's at home. Nobody's anywhere."

He had another reason for coming to town; he wanted to talk to Betsy. Try to. Betsy always went to her cabin for her noon meal, so he rode over there to wait. The rain started with a few drops, then a few more, and gradually picked up in volume until it was drumming steadily, making little puddles on the ground. Pettigrew couldn't invite himself inside Betsy's home, so he stood in his yellow slicker and waited, hanging onto the reins of his horse.

When she came she was wearing the same kind of slicker borrowed from the Canon City postmaster. That and a waterproof bonnet kept her dry. At the sight of Pettigrew she paused, then came on with her mouth set in a straight line. "Come in, Lem," is all she said.

He followed her inside, and started to apologize for the water dripping from his slicker and hat, but she said, "I won't offer you anything, because I don't want you to stay."

His chest went hollow and his shoulders slumped. "Why?"

She unbuttoned the slicker, took it off. He felt even hollower when he saw her trim figure in a dress that was pulled in at the middle. "You've killed again. It's all over town. You've earned a reputation as a killer. People are talking. 'Don't even look straight at Lem Pettigrew', they say. 'He'll shoot you down.' "

"It's . . ." He couldn't find the right words.

"You'll always have that reputation. I'm sorry, Lem. I really am sorry."

He tried to think of something to say. There was nothing more to be said. It was hopeless. "Goodbye, Betsy." He turned and went out the door.

She was right. He was a killer. As he rode east, following the Arkansas River, rain beating on his hat and shoulders, chilling his rein hand, he knew she was

179

right. Five men. He had a reputation now that would hound him as long as he stayed in Colorado. Everytime he rode down a street in Canon City, folks would recognize him, point at him, whisper. Decent folks would have nothing to do with him. If Betsy didn't believe in him, nobody would. A trial jury wouldn't believe him.

Lem Pettigrew rode in the rain, unmindful of the mud, the squishing of his horse's hooves, seeing nothing, hearing nothing. His hat was pulled low and his head was sucked down into his slicker. What had he gone and done, anyway? What he'd done was wreck any future he had in southern Colorado.

Beans had a fire going in the cookstove, and the warmth from it was good on a rainy day. "Guess what we're gonna eat for dinner," Beans said, cheerfully.

Though he felt anything but cheerful, Pettigrew tried to joke. "I couldn't guess in a million years. Wouldn't be beans, would it?"

"That's my name and that's my game."

Pettigrew said nothing, just slumped in a chair and stared at the floor.

"Somethin' wrong, partner?"

"Naw. Yeah."

"Wa-al, it's none of my business, I reckon."

Finally, Pettigrew heaved a long sigh and looked up. "How much money have you got?"

"A little over nine thousand."

"Would you pay eight thousand for this place?"

"How much've you got in it?"

"About eight thousand and a lot of sweat."

"You don't need to cheat yourself."

"I wouldn't be cheating myself. I owe you. Would you pay eight thousand?"

"In a minute, but you don't owe me anything."

"In my opinion, I do."

"Naw. The work I've been doin' here, well, if I buy

the outfit I will've been workin' for myself and you'll have been workin' for me."

"Huh," Pettigrew snorted with sarcasm. "It's almost funny the way things work out."

"You never know."

"You pay me eight thousand and you'll have enough left to get through the winter and maybe even hire somebody to help with the haying and the riding."

"Yup."

Pettigrew stood, walked into the bedroom, head down, turned on his heels and walked back. "If that's what you want we can go to the county recorder's office right now and close the deal."

"Fine with me, but let's eat first." The young cowboy tried to joke. "You know how much you like my beans."

Within four hours the deal was done. John Harvey Gipson had a recorded deed to a half-section of land and all improvements, seventy-four cows and their calves, ten bulls and three horses. Pettigrew had eight thousand dollars cash and a horse, saddle, bedroll and his clothes.

"Whatta ya say let's have a drink of whiskey," Beans said as they left the county office. "Ain't ever' day I buy a ranch."

"I'd like to, but I've got a badass reputation around here."

"Let's have a drink anyhow. If anydamnbody picks a fight with you he'll have to whup both of us."

For the first time that day, Pettigrew cracked a grin. They headed for the O.K. saloon. All activity ceased when they walked in. No one spoke, they only stared. Trying to ignore them, they stepped up to the long mahogany bar and ordered whiskey. "Partner," Beans said, after downing a shot, "I got to tell yu somethin'."

The whiskey felt warm and good in Pettigrew's stomach. "Fire away."

"It's a long story, but here goes: I was givin' some

181

serious thought to killin' you when I was sent to the pen, but the more I thought about it the more I begun to see things different. We was good friends, good partners. You was doin' what you was paid to do. By the time I got out I didn't wanta kill nobody. But I thought I oughtta do somethin' to get even."

He ordered another round from a grumpy bartender in a striped shirt with the sleeves rolled up. "That's why I come up here. But when I seen how poor you was and heered what kind of luck you was havin' I changed my mind about that too. Only . . ." He sipped at the second shot of whiskey. "Only, always somewhere in my head I thought I oughtta do somethin'. I felt like a debt had to be paid."

Pettigrew listened, very much interested. Beans went on: "Well, I done it."

"What did you done?"

"I got even with ya."

"How did you do that?"

"I stole your girl."

"Huh?"

"Now, don't get me wrong. I'm not usin' Betsy to get even. We just, uh, we just get along with each other, that's all. She's why I stuck around and come to town so much. She's why I bought your ranch."

"A-hum." Pettigrew had to clear his throat.

Beans set his empty glass on the bar with a clatter. "So whatta ya think of that?"

"Well, a-hum." Pettigrew managed to keep a straight face. "Well, like some wise old bird once said, 'All's fair in love and war'. I guess all I can say is congratulations. Betsy's a fine woman."

"You mad at me?"

"I ought to be, but . . . I guess the best man won." Pettigrew cracked his second grin of the day. "You got your revenge."

"It makes me feel a lot better. How about you?"

"Sure, uh, yeah, I guess this is how it ought to be."

And as he finished his whiskey, Pettigrew did feel better. It was a load off his mind. "Let's go back. I'll be off your property in the morning."

They went out onto the boardwalk, but they didn't get far. U.S. Marshal Dodds stepped out of a doorway and stood spraddle-legged in front of Pettigrew. Through his slit of a mouth, he said:

"All right, killer. Git in my office. I wanta talk to you."

Chapter Twenty-four

Beans started to follow them into the sheriff's combination office and jail, but Marshal Dodds growled at him. "Stay out. This's somethin' me and this gutshooter are gonna have to settle."

Beans said. "Need any help, Lem?"

"Naw. He's got nothing on me." He stepped inside, the marshal close behind him.

Marshal Dodds shut the door, latched it from the inside. He hitched his gun and holster into position. "Now then, you and me are gonna have a conversation, and I want straight answers."

Pettigrew could feel his face getting warm, his anger rising. "What's eating you now?"

"Another dead man, that's what. I'm a United States marshal and I've got jurisdiction everywhere. That suicide note over at Hardscrabble don't hold water. You killed that man and hid his body. You wrote the note, took his money and told the sheriff he killed himself."

"There was money in his cabin when I left."

"Sure, you left a few bucks to divert suspicion, but you took the rest, and you left his rifle 'cause you couldn't explain how a hoodlum like you come by it."

"That's crazy."

"Nope. You killed that man. You're a danger to society. I can't prove it just yet, but I will."

The anger that had been building for weeks suddenly

burst from Pettigrew. He hissed, "You're a God damn liar."

"That's it. I don't have to take insults. Turn around, killer, and I hope you resist arrest."

"No."

"What? What did you say?"

"I said no. Did anybody ever say no to you before?"

Marshal Dodds had his right hand on the walnut butt of his sixgun, ready to draw and shoot. With his left hand he grabbed Pettigrew by the shoulder and tried to turn him around. Pettigrew refused to be turned. He knew he had no chance in a fast draw contest, but he'd had enough of this lawman. One thought went through his mind: he was not going to be locked up again.

Through his slit of a mouth, the marshal said, "Don't ever say no to—" That was all he got out.

Pettigrew's left fist came up from thigh level and connected squarely with the marshal's jaw. All the strength in Pettigrew's arm and shoulder went into that punch, and the marshal staggered back, numb with shock. Before he stopped staggering, Pettigrew's right fist came up in a roundhouse swing and cracked him on the left temple. Then a left to the mouth and another right cross to the jaw. The lawman was staggering, stumbling, trying to draw his pistol. He got it only half out of its holster when another roundhouse right caught him on the left eye. He fell heavily. The sixgun dropped from his hand. Pettigrew picked up the pistol, cocked the hammer back and hissed:

"Get up, you son of a bitch. Get your sorry, trouble-making ass up from there. Get up or I'll stomp the hound dog shit out of you."

Marshal Dodds got to his hands and knees. Blood dripped from his nose onto the wooden floor. His flat-brim hat had rolled under the desk, and a long thin hank of hair hung over his face. A dark blue bruise under his left eye was swelling rapidly. Pettigrew hissed again. "Get up, God damn you. If I'm gonna be hung for a murder it'll be yours. Get your sorry, rotten ass up from there."

Slowly, the lawman stood, blood running down into his mouth. He flicked his tongue at it, and stood swaying like a drunken man, saying nothing.

But his slit eyes said DEATH. Death to any man who dared hit him.

The message was clear, and it brought another explosion of anger from Pettigrew.

A roundhouse left fist caught the marshal between the eyes with a sickening thud. The marshal dropped onto the seat of his pants.

Still, Pettigrew wasn't through. All the anger, disappointment and bitterness that had been simmering inside him was now boiling over. "I oughtta kill you," he said through tight jaws. "I oughtta put a slug in your guts and let you die an inch at a time. There's nothing worse than a bully with a badge."

The marshal dragged a shirt sleeve across his nose. The sleeve was bloody. He said nothing, but his eyes were no longer fixed on Pettigrew's face. Instead they were looking up the bore of his own gun.

For a long while, Pettigrew stood over him, pointing the sixgun at him. Then he stepped back. "Get on your feet. Maybe I'll let you live this time. Stand up, dammit it."

Again, the marshal got slowly to his feet, swaying. Pettigrew nodded at the open door between the office and jail. "Get in there. Move your ass, god-damn it."

"Mmph?" It came out as a mumble from numb swelling lips.

"Shut up. Get in there."

On unsteady legs, the marshal shuffled his feet through the door. The iron jail cell was also open, the long key in the lock. "Go on," Pettigrew ordered. More shuffling, and the marshal was inside. Pettigrew put a hand in the middle of his back and shoved him so hard he staggered across the cell, collided with the far wall and slid down it.

Marshal Dodds was no longer a tough, threatening, swaggering lawman. Instead, he was a beaten, bleeding mess cowering in a fetal position on the floor of his own jail.

Pettigrew slammed the door and locked it. He tested the door to make sure it was locked. "If the world is lucky, you'll starve before anybody finds you," he said.

He stuck the jail key in his hip pocket, threw the marshal's gun under the desk, unlatched the outer door and went outside, closing the door behind him. Beans was leaning against the building, waiting.

"I've got to get on my horse," Pettigrew said. "I've got to ride."

As they rode out of town on a high trot, Pettigrew's mouth was clamped shut, his jaw muscles bulged. Not until they were in the wagon ruts paralleling the river did Beans ask, "I reckon someday you'll tell me what happened."

He had to strain his ears to hear what Pettigrew said: "I hit the bastard." Pettigrew held out his right fist, displaying bloody knuckles. Speaking a little louder, he added, "I don't know who got hurt the worst, but he's locked up in his own jail and I'm not."

"Whoo. Partner, you better make yourself scarce. He'll have the whole damned U.S. Army after you."

"Yeah." Remembering the jail key, Pettigrew pulled it from his pocket and threw it into the Arkansas. "I don't know how long it will be before somebody finds him, and I don't know how long it will take them to get the jail door open, but I've got to git."

He picked the best horse he had, a bay gelding named Billy, put his eight thousand dollars in a leather money belt under his shirt, packed a change of clothes in his saddlebags. "I've got to travel light," he said.

"They'll be here lookin' for you. I'll tell 'em . . . lessee, I heard about a town up north called Leadville where men are swarmin' like a bunch of ants lookin' for gold or silver or lead or somethin'. I'll tell 'em you headed for Leadville. Let 'em look through that herd of humanity for you."

"Don't get in trouble on my account."

"I'll tell 'em you said you was goin' to Leadville. They can't prove you didn't say that."

Pettigrew stuck out his hand to shake. "Give my regards to Betsy." They shook, and Pettigrew spun his horse and rode away. Riding east at a high trot, following the Arkansas River, Pettigrew had a strong urge to look back, back to the place where he'd planned to build a future, where he'd worked hard to build a future. But with determination, he kept his gaze fixed straight ahead.

"To hell with everything," he muttered.

The road to Pueblo was well-used. It was the stagecoach route. Pettigrew didn't want anyone to tell Marshal Dodds they'd seen him, so he crossed the river at the first crossing place he came to and stayed out of sight of the road. He approached the town in the dark from the south, and told the night man at the Pueblo Livery he'd come from Trinidad. As he walked to a working man's hotel, carrying his saddle bags on his left shoulder, he thanked the stars that he hadn't branded his horses and had depended on bills of sale to prove ownership. A Rafter 4 brand on the bay gelding would have told a lawman he was in town. The horse's color would cause no suspicion. Most horses were bays. At the hotel he signed the register as George Jackson from Trinidad. Maybe he'd have a few days before the lawmen tracked him here.

In the morning he shaved in cold water, wiped his face dry with a strip of muslin which passed for a towel and combed his hair. He considered leaving his money belt in the room, but after testing the lock and finding it weak, he strapped it around his waist. The belt and its full pockets created a bulge under his shirt. He wished he'd had a coat of some kind to hide the bulge, but he was traveling light.

For breakfast in the Arkansaw Cafe he had hotcakes, eggs, ham and coffee. At least he would eat well before he was locked up again. He had a decision to make.

He wanted to see Sheriff Bowen. The sheriff could tell him about that court order and who took the money. He could tell him which judge signed the order, if a judge did sign it. That kind of information could come in handy. But the sheriff would also know he was in town, and he'd hear sooner or later that he was wanted in Canon City. That wouldn't do.

It was early, too early for the stores to open. A change of clothes and a new hat would make him harder to recognize. He'd attend to that as soon as the haberdasheries opened. Meanwhile, he walked to the brick courthouse, idly curious, and was surprised to find the door unlocked. Inside, he was alone in a corridor lined with doors with frosted glass panes. On the far wall, in a small glass cage, was a building directory. Pettigrew read as far down the list of county and state offices as the Colorado State District Court. There was only one, and the judge was The Honourable George Walls. The judge was another public official who would recognize him. Well, he mused to himself outside, he didn't want to talk to the judge anyway. He wondered which judge signed a certain court order — if it even was signed by a judge.

When Miller & Son's Fine Clothiers opened its doors Pettigrew was the first customer. An hour later he was heading for his hotel, carrying an armload of packages. In another hour he came out of the hotel, wearing a dark fingerlength coat, wool pants with creases down the legs, a pale blue shirt and a black string tie. He'd tried a wide necktie, but couldn't figure out how to tie it and didn't want the clothier to know he was that ignorant. His hat was another Stetson, grey, with a flat wide brim and a round crown. The brand new hat and his scuffed boots were a dead giveaway — he was a cattleman in from the hills trying to look like a city slicker. Well, he could do something about that.

In an alley behind the hotel, he took a careful look in both directions, then threw the hat on the ground and stomped it flat. When he straightened it and rubbed in a smudge of dirt, it no longer looked brand new. "I must look a pure fool," he said to himself as he put the hat back on. Then he went looking for a boot shop.

Cynthia Atkinson wouldn't open her hotel room door for just anybody, but she recognized his name and voice and opened the door. For a few seconds she didn't recognize him.

"Why, you look, uh, almost like a . . ."

"Dumb hick from the sticks," Pettigrew finished for her. He entered and closed the door behind him.

She stood back, pinched her chin with her right thumb and forefinger, and let her brown eyes rove over him. "Well, you could pass for a construction engineer. I mean, you obviously are an outdoorsman."

With a wry grin, he said, "Nah. I'm what you city folks call a country bumpkin, and you know something? I don't care."

A wide smile spread over her face. "You'd be surprised, Lem, at how many Chicago ladies are intrigued by the outdoor type. Especially men from out West. You'd have them fawning all over you."

He had to chuckle. "They'd scare hell out of me."

"Oh, I suspect you'd become accustomed to it."

"Well, anyway, let's go pay our respects to that lawyer."

This time Everett Clawson, Attorney At Law, was in. But he wasn't seeing anyone. "Mr. Clawson is due in court very soon," his pretty young receptionist said. "He is very busy."

Pettigrew and Mrs. Atkinson stood before her desk in an outer office. "We only need a minute of his time," Pettigrew said.

"It's very important," Cynthia Atkinson said.

"Tell him Mrs. George Atkinson wants to see him," said Pettigrew.

The receptionist stood, showing a trim figure in a

long pink frilly dress. "I'll tell him, but I'm afraid he hasn't time to see anyone this morning."

She opened the door to the lawyer's inner sanctum only wide enough to slip through. In twenty seconds she was back. "Mr. Clawson will see you, but only for a moment." This time she opened the door wider.

Everett Clawson was a fine looking man. Tall, straight, well-dressed in a dark suit and necktie, he had thick dark hair parted in the middle and a neatly trimmed dark moustache. He got to his feet behind a big mahogany desk when they entered, and for a half-second his grey eyes under thick eyebrows narrowed. Only for a flicker.

"Why," he said in a masculine voice that could be clearly heard in a large courtroom, "it's Miss — uh, I expected Mrs. Atkinson."

"That is how I am known in Colorado, Mr. Clawson." She didn't blink an eye.

"Well, I have only a minute before I'm due in court. What can I do for you?"

Cynthia Atkinson turned to Pettigrew. "You tell him, Lem."

Pettigrew guessed it would be useless to try to be subtle with this man. He was blunt. "We want the fifty thousand dollars you confiscated from Mrs. Atkinson here."

The lawyer's expression changed to perplexed. "What fifty thousand dollars are you referring to?"

"You know," Pettigrew said. "And we know you know."

Chapter Twenty-five

One side of the lawyer's office was lined with handsomely bound law books. A tall grandfather clock stood in a corner. Two chairs with padded leather seats sat in front of the desk. No one was sitting. The only sound to be heard was the clock ticking; in the heavy silence it was like thunder.

Lawyer Clawson stared at Pettigrew for a moment, then quickly picked up a leather briefcase from the desk and hurried around him and Mrs. Atkinson to the door. "I have no idea what you are talking about," he said, holding the door open for them. "You must excuse me. I'm in the middle of some very important litigation concerning the Atchison, Topeka and Santa Fe versus the Denver and Rio Grande. Millions of dollars are at stake here. You can understand why I must ask you to leave."

What could he do, Pettigrew asked himself. Wrestle the man to the floor and make him listen? No, but he'd be damned if he'd be flamboozled by this dandy, either. He gently took Mrs. Atkinson's elbow in his right hand and escorted her through the door. To Lawyer Clawson he said,

"We'll meet again. You can bet on it."

A whistle scream split the quiet morning as a steam engine shuffled cars in the railroad yards. Horse-drawn traffic was heavy on the streets. Pueblo was a bustling town. Mrs. Atkinson said, "I know about the legal battle between the two railroads. Each wants the right to build tracks through the Royal Gorge. It's the only route through the mountains to all that mineral wealth in the north and northwest. I've heard Mr. Atkinson talk about it. Mr. Clawson is right — it's worth millions of dollars."

"And the lawyers who win in court will be well paid."

"Very well. Very well indeed."

"Hmm."

"What are we going to do now, Lem?"

Pettigrew faced her in front of the lawyer's office. "We're not gonna let that gent get rid of us." He studied his new boots a moment. "I would like to know more about this mess. But, uh, Mrs. Atkinson — Cynthia, I'm in trouble with the law. I beat up a United States marshal in Canon City, and I can't go to the sheriff myself. Can you . . . I'd like to know for sure what became of the money, whether the sheriff took it. I'd bet anything he didn't, but I'd like to know for sure. Can you go ask him? Don't tell him it wasn't in the inventory of Mr. Atkinson's property."

"I understand. I'll try to think of a way to put the question without arousing suspicion. I'm not quite sure how I'll do it, but I'll try to think of a way." She turned toward the courthouse, then stopped suddenly. "You beat up a United States marshal?"

Shaking his head, Pettigrew said, "I'm always in trouble, ain't I? I don't guess there's any use trying to explain how it happened. I, uh, maybe I am to blame, at least partly. I don't know."

"That's why you're dressed differently. You're afraid of being recognized."

"Yes. That's right. If I'm arrested, you don't know anything about what happened at Canon City."

"No. But please don't be arrested." She lifted her skirts above her shoe tops with one hand and walked down the boardwalk.

Pettigrew stayed where he was a moment, thinking.

Then he turned and went back inside the lawyer's office. "Miss, would you tell me please which bank in Denver Mr. Clawson does business with?"

A worry frown pinched her eyebrows together. "I, uh, sir, I don't believe Mr. Clawson would, uh, I'm afraid I shouldn't tell you."

"All right. Don't get in trouble on my account. We can find out by sending some telegraphs. I just thought you might save us some time."

"I'm sorry, sir." The young woman appeared visibly uncomfortable.

"Thanks anyway."

He met Mrs. Atkinson in the lobby of her hotel, standing when she came in. She sat in a upholstered chair next to his. "What I suspected was correct. Sheriff Bowen, I gathered, is not very sophisticated, and he let a smooth-talking lawyer take the money. Mr. Clawson told him he was going to turn it over to the court. I asked him whether he read the court order carefully, and he said he did. I doubt he did, but he probably did read the judge's signature. He said it was a Judge Walls."

"Did your questions make him suspicious?"

"A little. But I made him think I am trying to find a legal way to claim some of Mr. Atkinson's estate. He advised me to go to a lawyer. As I said, Sheriff Bowen isn't very sophisticated."

"All right," Pettigrew said, "we already knew the lawyer didn't turn the money over to the court, and now we know he didn't leave it with the sheriff. I'll bet it's in a bank in Denver. Do you know of any way we can find out which bank?"

"No . . ." She frowned. "I do know from listening to conversations involving Mr. Atkinson that banks will not disclose the amount of funds in anyone's account. That is confidential. But I also recall Mr. Atkinson once wiring a bank in Chicago to ascertain whether a draft drawn on that bank by a certain individual could be redeemed."

"In other words, whether the individual was good for it."

"Exactly."

"Can we do that from here? I mean wire the banks in Denver?"

"I suppose we can. Yes, I believe we can. At least it's worth a try."

"You know the kind of lingo big businessmen use. Can you send some telegraphs? We don't know which bank, but I'd guess it's one of the big ones. Say, the First National or the Denver National."

She stood. "I'll do it."

It was noon, but they wasted no time going to the telegraph desk in the AT&SF depot. Mrs. Atkinson's face screwed up in thought as she wrote the messages on sheets of yellow paper. Addressed to the cashier, the messages read: "Sir, I have been offered a check in the amount of fifty thousand dollars to be drawn on the account of Everett Clawson of Pueblo, Colo. I must learn as soon as possible whether the check will be honored at your institution. Please advise. Signed Mrs. Charles B. Atkinson."

"There," she said. "I hope this is composed in a business-like manner."

The telegrapher, a scrawny man wearing a green eyeshade and garters on his sleeves, read both messages. "You wanta send the same message to both banks?"

"Yes sir, I do."

Shrugging, the telegrapher said, "O.K."

"Now," she said to Pettigrew, "how about some lunch?"

"My stomach has been telling me it's dinner time," he said.

At five o'clock no answer had come at the telegraph desk, and they knew they'd have to wait until morning. Waiting made Pettigrew uncomfortable. He bought a newspaper and went to his hotel. It was a relief to get that damned string tie and coat off and also that heavy money belt. He read the newspaper, found no reference to his altercation in Canon City, then, with nothing else to do, again counted the money in the money belt.

By mid-morning both telegrams had been answered. The cashier at the Denver National Bank said Mr. Clawson had no account there. But the answer from the First National Bank's cashier read: "A check in the amount of fifty thousand dollars drawn on the account of Everett Clawson can be redeemed when properly processed."

"We don't have to guess now," said Pettigrew.

"Now we know," said Mrs. Atkinson.

But again they had to wait. The lawyer was in court. "Know what I'm gonna do?" Pettigrew said. "I'm gonna go over to the courtroom and sit there and stare at Everett Clawson. Just sit and stare at him."

"That will make him so nervous that he'll want to be rid of us. In fact, that is an excellent idea. I'll go with you."

It didn't work.

Attorney Clawson was standing behind a table arguing in legal jargon and didn't notice the two at first. Then he happened to look over the handful of spectators and did a double take. Pettigrew's face was expressionless. Mrs. Atkinson smiled and nodded. If the lawyer was bothered by their presence he didn't show it. Pettigrew had to admire the man's performance. When the judge banged his gavel and said the court would be adjourned until nine a.m. tomorrow, Pettigrew went up to him.

"Where do you want to talk, here or in private?"

Clawson was putting papers inside his briefcase. He didn't even look up. "Sir . . . Mr. Pettigrew, isn't it? I don't believe we have anything to talk about."

"You talk to us or you talk to the judge."

He looked up, then. "Very well, meet me in my office, in oh, say ten minutes."

"Make it five minutes."

They waited twenty minutes, and all the time Pettigrew was thinking: That son of a bitch is making us wait on purpose. He wants us to think he's not even a little bit worried about what we've got to say. It's about time somebody cut his water off.

Lawyer Clawson, when he came in, was in a hurry. "I can spare very little time. I have work to do." He went into his inner office. Pettigrew and Mrs. Atkinson followed. They were not invited to sit.

Standing with his feet apart, thumbs hooked in his gunbelt, Pettigrew said, "Here's the way it is. You knew about the fifty thousand dollars ransom that Mrs. Atkinson was keeping in the hotel safe. You've got ears in all the right places. You either got a court order or you faked one to get your hands on the late Charles Atkinson's assets, including the cash. To make it easy you got the sheriff to serve it. That's what you did. What you didn't do was turn the money over to the authorities."

The lawyer was seated behind his desk, shuffling papers, appearing to pay little attention to what Pettigrew was saying. Now he looked from under his thick eyebrows. "I have no idea what you are talking about."

"All right," Pettigrew said, "I'll bet the judge knows nothing about the cash. But the sheriff saw you take it, and when he gets done telling the judge about it, you're gonna be hauled before the court yourself—as a defendant."

Mrs. Atkinson added, "You can't account for the money. Either you turn it over to us or you turn it over to the court and admit you converted it to your own use."

The paper shuffling stopped. The lawyer's expression changed from one of annoyance to a hint of fear. "What . . . ?" His mouth stayed open a moment. "I don't have the money," he said finally.

"Sure you do," Pettigrew said. "You put it in a separate bank account in Denver. The First National Bank."

"How do you . . . ? Uh, it is part of the late Charles B. Atkinson's estate."

"Supposed to be. But there's no record of it."

"This," Mrs. Atkinson said, "looks very, very bad. It will ruin your career."

"And you're in the middle of a million dollar case," Pettigrew observed sympathetically.

Clawson's composure was fading. A small strangling sound came from his throat. "What, uh, what do you expect me to do?"

"Simple," Pettigrew said. "Give the money back to Mrs. Atkinson, and no more will be said about it."

"This is blackmail! You're a pair of thieves."

Pettigrew's voice grew hard, razor sharp, "All right, that's enough of your bull. Excuse my language, Mrs. Atkinson, but I've looked at this jackass's face as long as I care to. Mister, we want that money and we want it by this time tomorrow."

Clearing his throat, Clawson asked, "A-hem, what will you do?"

Pettigrew said, "Guess."

Chapter Twenty-six

The boardwalk was so crowded that men often stepped off it and onto the street to make room for the ladies. A few tipped their hats at the beautiful Mrs. Atkinson. Even the laboring men gave her room. She smiled graciously and repeatedly said, "Thank you, sir." But when she spoke to Pettigrew, she wasn't smiling. "What do you think he'll do?"

"Nothing, probably. Not right away. I don't think we've convinced him yet."

"What else can we do?"

"We have to find a way to let him know we're deadly serious, remind him that we can shoot down his law practice and have him convicted of a crime."

"How can we do that?"

"Show up in the courtroom again in the morning. Try to make him sweat."

"He did lose some of his stuffy composure in his office."

"Yeah, he's worried, but maybe not worried enough yet."

She asked him to have dinner with her. "A lady dining alone attracts the kind of attention I do not care for." He had to excuse himself, go to the men's water closet and take a bill out of his money belt to pay for their meal. They took their time, had a second cup of coffee, and lingered over apple pie. Then he escorted her to her room and left.

It was dusk when he decided to walk to the livery barn and see that his bay horse was cared for. Besides, it was cool outside, and his hotel room was stifling. He wished he could put on his old clothes, but was afraid he'd be too easy to recognize. By now Marshal Dodds had to have gotten word to every lawman in Southern Colorado to be on the lookout for Lemual Pettigrew. Walking to the livery barn, he wondered how Beans Gipson had been treated by the marshal. Beans was like Pettigrew — he'd put up with the marshal's bully boy ways for a while, but not for long. He wondered, too, when Beans and Betsy would be married. She'd be a good wife, and Beans, while he liked a beer or a shot of whiskey now an then, wasn't the kind to carouse much.

Those were the thoughts going through Pettigrew's mind when he walked into the alley of the barn. The alley divided two rows of box stalls from one end of the barn to the other. The hostler wasn't there. Pettigrew should have come earlier. Now it was too dark to find his horse. He was looking for a lantern when he noticed a man standing outlined in the door. The man had a gun in his hand. He raised his hand and pointed the gun at Pettigrew.

Cursing his own foolishness, Pettigrew threw himself to his left and down onto the cool dirt floor. The gun spat flame. The explosion rocked the barn. Horses snorted and jumped in their box stalls. The lead slug thunked into the floor near Pettigrew's head.

Immediately Pettigrew had the Colt in his hand, but the shooter was no fool. He'd disappeared from the door where he could be seen in the pale light from outside. It was black inside. Pettigrew could see nothing to shoot at.

He'd been through all this so many times in the past few weeks that he felt little fear. Just weariness. How much could a man stand? How many bullets could a man dodge before one found him? Grumbling inwardly, he knew he had had enough. But he stayed still.

Only the horses moved, snorting and stomping. Trying to think of a way out, Pettigrew remembered two entrances, one on each end of the barn. If he could somehow back out of the other end, he could disappear himself. Nope. He saw, when he looked over his shoulder, that the other end was blocked. Another man with a gun was outlined in it. That man, too, stepped inside into the darkness.

He wanted to shoot back, but the flash from his Colt would show the two gunslingers where he was, and between the two of them they could pour enough lead in his direction that they couldn't miss.

That's what they tried to do anyway.

Gunshots came fast and furious. Bullets slammed into the dirt floor. Then one of the men hollered, "Shoot low, God damn it, I'm over here."

Shoot low. Sure. Riddle the floor with lead. Riddle everything on the floor. Get up, Lem Pettigrew. Get your ass off the floor.

Reaching up with one hand, groping, he found that he was next to the half-door of a stall. Without taking time to think about it, he stood, crawled quickly over the top of the door, and dropped headfirst inside the stall. A horse snorted, squealed and kicked the wall on the other end.

Damn, the horse's carrying on would show them which stall he was in. Well, they couldn't see him any better than he could see them. But then, dammit, they didn't have to see him. They could step up to the stall, flatten themselves against the outside wall where they'd be poor targets and pour fire into the stall until they killed everything in it. The horse mattered not one damn bit.

Hell, they might not have to kill him. All the gunfire and the sight of a man on his knees had the horse crazy with fear. It might stomp him to death.

Feeling boxed in, Pettigrew considered trying to get on the other side of the horse, keep it between him and the stall door. No. If he accidentally touched the wrong end of the horse in the dark he'd be kicked to pieces. What, then? He remembered the barn was two stories high. Probably a hay loft overhead. Yeah, and the ladder wasn't more than two stalls away. It would be on his right as he went out the stall door. But would he be any better off in the loft? And how in hell could he get up that ladder without being shot? Naw, that wasn't a good idea either.

They were whispering. "He's in one a these stalls."

"Yeah, in that 'un where the horse is raisin' a ruckus."

"Be careful, God damn it. Don't shoot me by mistake."

They were coming. Any second now the air inside the stall would be full of lead. He could shoot back at their muzzle flashes, and maybe get one man. But between them they'd get him. He had to move.

Groping with his left hand, Pettigrew found the latch on the outside of the half-door. He unlatched it and stepped back. The horse saw the opening and stampeded out.

Guns boomed. Gun muzzles flashed. A horse squealed. Pettigrew ducked out. He knew from the sounds that the horse had run to his right. He turned left, and ran toward the end of the barn. He collided with something soft. A man grunted, swore. A gun fired near his left ear. He fired the Colt. Thumbed the hammer back and fired again. The bulk in front of him dropped. Now the other man was shooting. Pettigrew yelled, "Hey, God damn it, I'm over here."

The shooting stopped. Pettigrew ran out of the barn and kept running until he was near the lamplight of a downtown street. His left ear was ringing like a church bell. Holstering his gun under the fingerlength coat, Pettigrew tried to slow his breathing. A few pedestrians were on the street, and a one-horse buggy went by in the opposite direction. Two men standing under a street lamp were looking his way. He tried to appear calm.

"Hey, mister," one said, "what was all that shootin'

202

about over there?"

"I don't know," Pettigrew said. "I heard it too. I got the hell away from there." He lifted his hat, ran his fingers through his hair and reset the hat. "Sounded like it came from the livery." He tugged the coat down, made sure it covered the Colt, then walked toward his hotel, hoping the men wouldn't run for the sheriff.

I was a fool, he said under his breath. Fool, hell, I was plain stupid. I should have known Everett Clawson would try to have me killed. Sure, that was his only defense. Kill us. Hire a couple of town toughs to shut our mouths. And I walked right into their trap.

He stopped suddenly. Kill *us*. Both of us. He has to shut up both of us.

Trying not to run and draw attention to himself, walking as fast as he could, he made his way to the Pueblo Hotel. In the lobby, he asked the bespectacled desk clerk, "Is Mrs. Atkinson in her room?" Without waiting for an answer, he went up the stairs two at a time.

"But sir . . ."

Pettigrew was already tapping lightly on her door. No answer. He cursed under his breath. Damned, stupid cowpuncher. Why didn't you use your goddam head? Tapped again.

The desk clerk was coming up the stairs behind him. "Sir, we can't have . . ." Pettigrew ignored him, tapped again. Let out his breath with a sigh when she answered. "Yes?"

"It's Lem," he said. "Are you — is everything all right?" To the clerk he said, "I just want to talk to her a minute, then I'll leave."

The door opened a crack, and he could see her, all silky-gowned and tousel haired. "Lem, is something wrong?"

"No, uh . . ." Glancing at the clerk, he went on. "I just wanted to be sure you got here safe. I think you'd better not open the door to anybody. Not anybody, understand?"

203

"Why yes? Did something happen?"

"No. I wanted to be sure you're safe, that's all. Keep your door locked. I'll see you in the morning." To the bug-eyed clerk he asked, "Have you got good locks on these doors?"

"Yes, sir. The doors are solid oak with deadbolt locks."

"Good. Keep an eye on this one, will you?"

"Of course, sir."

"Good man."

It was in the newspaper. A black headline read: "SHOOTING AT LIVERY BARN." A smaller sub-head under it read: "Man Dead At Scene." Another subhead under that one read: "Horse Also Killed." Reading down, Pettigrew's eyes finally came to the story:

Pueblo City Marshal John Greenlee, answering reports of gunshots at the Pueblo Livery shortly after dark last night, found a man dead of a gunshot wound to the chest. Marshal Greenlee stated that while examining the scene by lantern light he found numerous bullet holes in the walls, which indicated that a gun battle had taken place. The deceased's pistol had only one live cartridge in it. A chestnut mare belonging to a local merchant was found so severely wounded from a gunshot that the animal had to be destroyed.

Marshal Greenlee speculated that the deceased, who was unidentified as this newspaper went to press, had an argument over a horse with a person or persons unknown and the argument ended in gunfire.

Pettigrew was relieved to find no mention of a man seen running from the direction of the barn. Too bad about that horse, though. The town marshal was probably asking questions of the horse's owner about now. Hope the gent, whoever he is, has a good alibi.

Mrs. Atkinson had heeded Pettigrew's advice, and hadn't come down for breakfast. Only after she recognized his voice did she unlock the door and open it. "What happened?" she asked, stepping back to allow him in. "Something must have happened." She was dressed for the street in a pink shirtwaist with large mother-of-pearl buttons and a long grey skirt.

He told her about it. "I guess I'm not in danger of being arrested for this shooting," he said. "But . . ."

"But what, Lem?"

"That's another man dead. I'm beginning to lose count."

"They tried to kill you."

Glumly, he said, "Yeah, sure."

He waited in the restaurant while she visited the ladies' water closet, then stood when she entered. He had his favorite breakfast of coffee, hotcakes, ham and eggs. She had toast, marmalade and coffee. They got to the courtroom before the hearing was resumed, and drew fearful glances from Everett Clawson. A wrought iron railing separated the spectators from the lawyers' tables and lectern, but Pettigrew stepped through the swinging gate. He walked boldly up to Clawson, and spoke one word:

"Now."

Chapter Twenty-seven

"Your Honor." Lawyer Clawson buttoned his grey suit coat and shot his cuffs as he stood. A silver cufflink gleamed briefly in the sunlight coming through the high, third-floor window. He stood at the lectern and addressed the court. "Your Honor, I must respectfully request a continuance of this matter. Something urgent and unexpected has come up, and I have no choice but to attend to it immediately."

Counsel for the other side opposed a continuance, but Judge Wall read the desperation in Clawson's voice and face and granted a delay of two days. Bang, went his gavel, and he rose, gathered his black robe around him and walked in a dignified manner through the rear door.

A man behind Pettigrew said, "Hell, the judge wanted to go fishin' anyway."

In the corridor, Clawson whispered, "All right. I'll wire the bank. But I'll have to go to Denver, and there won't be a train north until tonight."

"We'll expect you back tomorrow," Pettigrew said. "If you're not on the southbound train tomorrow you'd better not come back."

Mrs. Atkinson added, "We know you were behind the shooting last night."

Clawson was outraged. "I most certainly was not. I had nothing whatever to do with that."

"Sure, sure," Pettigrew said.

It was a long day. Pettigrew didn't want to spend any more time in public places than he had to, so he stayed in his room, going out only to eat lunch. He even begged off having dinner with Mrs. Atkinson. She understood.

"But don't leave the hotel," Pettigrew warned. "And don't open the door without knowing for sure who's out there."

At dusk, he heard the scream of a steam whistle and guessed the northbound was ready to pull out. Wearing his long coat over his sixgun, he strolled to the depot. Yes, Clawson was boarding the one Pullman coach, carrying two leather valises. The steam whistle screamed twice more, a conductor in a black bill cap said, " 'Bo-oard," then picked up the iron stool used for a step and climbed into the coach. Dirty black smoke puffed from the big engine's smokestack, the engine's drive wheels spun on the rails, and soon the long train was moving, gradually picking up speed.

Again Mrs. Atkinson refused to open her hotel room door until he repeated his name twice. Again he waited for her in the hotel dining room. While they ate breakfast, she had a suggestion:

"Have you ever heard of San Francisco, California, Lem?"

"I've heard of it."

"I've never been there, but I've been told it's a wonderfully exciting city. The temperature is always warm, the ocean is beautiful, and there are some wonderful hotels and restaurants. Wouldn't that be a great place to go from here? And one can travel all the way by rail. There are sleeping cars and dining cars, and all the comforts of a hotel."

Pettigrew drained his coffee cup. "Yeah, I met a gent once that had been there."

"Would you like to go there? With me?"

He almost choked on his coffee. "What? With you?"

"Do you think you could stand a vacation with me? You are in danger of being arrested if you stay in Southern Colorado."

"Why, uh, a-hem, I, uh . . . I think that would be, uh . . ."

"We can take the train to Denver tonight then plan an itinerary from there."

"Yeah, yes. I think that would be fine."

A small frown brought a crease between her brown eyes. "You're not sure. You need to think it over."

"Well, that's something I never thought of. You're right, I have to get out of Southern Colorado. Maybe . . . maybe your plan is a good one."

"Let's not waste any time. Let's take the train to Denver tonight."

"Sure, but we'll have to get our hands on that money first."

"If we don't get it by tonight, perhaps we'll have to plan on not getting it at all."

"We'll get it. The only thing that worries me is the train from the north is supposed to get in here about two-thirty. I don't know when it leaves Denver, and I don't know when the banks in Denver open. Old Clawson might have to rattle his hocks to get to the bank and get on the train."

"I think he'll try. The judge gave him only two days. Do you think it would be safe to greet him at the depot?"

"That's as good a place as any."

The southbound Denver & Rio Grande was forty-five minutes late. While they waited in the Pueblo depot, Pettigrew studied the faces of all the men in the room. He saw no one who looked dangerous, but he knew from experience that most of the most dangerous men in the world looked like gentlemen. When the train whistled its approach, everyone got up from the long wooden benches and went outside to watch it come. Pettigrew and Mrs. Atkinson waited inside, watching through a window.

With a lot of hissing, steaming and puffing, the train screeched to a stop with the passenger coach right in front of the depot. The conductor was the first out, placing the iron stool in front of the coach steps. Passengers followed. Some were greeted with hugs and kisses from relatives. Some were businessmen who had no one to greet them. Everett Clawson was one of the last out, carrying the two valises.

Pettigrew wasted no time. "Which one is the money in?" Pettigrew asked, stepping in front of him. Mrs. Atkinson was behind Pettigrew.

"Why, uh." The lawyer's eyes were nervous. "See here, you can't just take it here, now."

"No use waiting. Which one?"

"This one. See here, do you swear you won't mention this to anyone?"

"Not if the money is all here."

"It's here. Do you give me your word absolutely?"

"Yeah, and my word is better than yours any day." Pettigrew took one of the valises from Clawson's hand, unlatched it, opened it a crack. "All right, we'll go someplace and count the money. If it's all here, you won't see or hear from us again. That's a promise."

Everett Clawson, Attorney At Law, was no longer a tall, dignified, professional man. He had suddenly shrunk, was stoop-shouldered and ready to cry. Pettigrew and Mrs. Atkinson left him standing there, looking like a lost child.

In the hotel room, Pettigrew opened the valise and dumped the money on the bed. He had to suck in his breath at the sight of it. The woman said, "M-my goodness." They spent the next twenty minutes counting.

"I never in my life," said Pettigrew, "thought I would have so much money that it would take more than one minute to count it."

"There are forty bundles," she said. "Each bundle

contains twenty-five fifty dollar bills."

"And most of them aren't new. They've been around."

"Of course. An attorney wouldn't accept ransom money that could be traced."

"Whoo. Boy, oh, boy."

"Money!" Cynthia hugged bundles of money to her breasts. "It's wonderful! It's terrific! There's nothing like money!"

"A-hem." Pettigrew got hold of his emotions. "All right. Now. Let's go back to the depot and buy two tickets to Denver."

"Yes. You're absolutely right. Let's not waste any time in his town."

"Tell you what, I'll go buy the tickets. You stay here. Lock the door behind me and don't open it 'til you hear my voice."

"Yes. I'll do exactly that."

He couldn't help feeling uneasy as he walked back to the depot. He had a feeling he was being watched. Stopping, pretending to grope through his pockets, he looked back, studied the people behind him. No one paid him any attention. At the depot he bought two tickets for the northbound to Denver, then, walking fast, got back on the busy streets. A display of men's clothing in a store window gave him an excuse to stop and study his backtrail again. He saw no one suspicious. Still, knowing that he and the woman had beat a lawyer out of fifty thousand dollars made him nervous. Everett Clawson had hired two men to kill him. He'd try again. Where and how would they do it? On the street? In the hotel?

Pettigrew owned a good horse and saddle, and they could be sold for around a hundred dollars. That is if he could arrange a sale. It would have to be a quick sale. He turned his steps toward the livery barn, went two blocks, stopped. From where he stood, under a canvas awning in front of a hardware store, he could see a man with a star pinned to his shirt talking to the

210

livery hostler. Still trying to figure out what had happened, no doubt.

Stay away from there, Lem Pettigrew, he told himself. So you'll loose a horse and saddle. That's better than losing your freedom. Especially now that he had money to spend. He turned and went to his hotel, packed his saddle bags, threw them over his left shoulder, and went to her hotel.

She opened the door after he identified himself, then locked it behind him. He showed her the tickets, and sat in one of the chairs.

"Oh, I wish we could catch a train to Denver right now," she said. "This waiting is awful. I've spent entirely too much time waiting lately."

"I think I'll stay right here 'til train time," Pettigrew said. "Can we send for something to eat?"

"I'm too excited to eat. Perhaps we can buy some sandwiches on the train."

"Probably a good idea to stay in this room."

"Well, I, . . . do have to, this is embarrassing."

"What? Oh. I getcha. All right, I'll stand in the hall and wait for you. Nobody's gonna rob me when I've got a gun in my hand."

That's what they did. He kept the Colt in his hand while she visited the ladies' water closet, and he stood at the top of the stairs while she ordered sandwiches from the hotel restaurant. They ate in her room. He listened carefully everytime someone came up the stairs and walked down the hall, half-expecting a knock on the door.

She was right. Waiting was awful. She packed and repacked two leather suitcases. She asked, "How are we going to carry all this?"

"I can carry the suitcases, but . . ." He didn't want to tell her of his fears, but on second thought, maybe she ought to know. "To tell you the truth, Cynthia, I'd kind of like to keep my right hand free."

"Why?" Then her eyes widened. "Oh, I see. Do you

211

think he'll try again?"

"I wouldn't put anything past him."

"Oh. Well then, I'll have to take only one piece of luggage. I'll have to leave a few articles of clothing and a good quality case behind, but those are small items compared to what we have in that valise."

"I'm leaving behind a good horse and saddle. The livery owner will sell them when I don't show up."

"That's a shame, but just think of what we are not leaving behind."

He grinned. "I am thinking about that."

Not until they heard the steam whistle announce the arrival of the northbound train did they leave the hotel. She carried the valise full of money. He carried his saddlebags over his left shoulder and her one suitcase in his left hand.

Now that the railroad ran north and south along Colorado's Front Range folks were traveling more. The Pullman coach was almost full of travelers when Pettigrew and the woman found seats near the middle. She took the inside seat, while he sat on the aisle. They put their baggage in an overhead rack—except for the valise. That they kept on the floor between them.

Pettigrew was wary. He couldn't believe Everett Clawson would allow them to leave town without another try. The lawyer would do anything, kill both of them, for fifty thousand dollars. Anything but wreck his career. Pettigrew studied the face of every man who walked the aisle of the coach. He wished the damned train would get moving.

Finally it did. The whistle screeched, and the conductor hollered, " 'Bo-oard," and picked up the iron stool. Puffs of hissing steam came from the boiler, the drive wheels spun, and the train started moving. Pettigrew sighed with relief and leaned back on the wooden seat. At last.

Suddenly he jerked upright again. "Oh, no," he groaned.

"What is it, Lem?" Fear was in her voice. "Is something wrong?"

He had seen them. Two men, wearing wide-brim hats, black silk bandanas around their necks, baggy wool pants and jackboots. They had been just standing there watching people board, looking innocent. Now they were pulling the bandanas up over their faces.

Jaws tight, Pettigrew said, "Stay here. No matter what happens, stay here."

Chapter Twenty-eight

The train was moving slowly when Pettigrew half-ran toward the back of the coach to the door. The door was opening inward. By the time Pettigrew got there one man was inside and the other was standing on the iron steps ready to climb in. Both men had sixguns in their hands. The first one saw Pettigrew coming, and fired hastily. A woman seated near the door screamed. The bullet zinged past Pettigrew's left ear and smashed through the coach wall on the opposite side. Pettigrew grabbed at his own gun. The damned long coat got in the way. The shooter was thumbing the hammer back, ready to shoot again. Too late, Pettigrew knew.

Lowering his left shoulder, he rammed the first man in the chest, knocking him backwards. Another shot boomed. A bullet tore a hole in the ceiling. Pettigrew rammed him again, still trying to get his Colt untangled from the long coat tail. The train was picking up speed.

Women were screaming. Men were cursing. A gent in cattleman's clothes ran up behind Pettigrew, a sixgun in his hand, ready to shoot at a masked man. He couldn't get around Pettigrew to get a clear shot.

Pettigrew got his Colt free, but his running and ramming had him off balance. And the gunman he'd collided with was teetering in the doorway, pulling on the front of Pettigrew's coat, trying to keep his own balance. Pettigrew was falling. Both the masked men had

214

tumbled back out of the door now. The first one lost his grip on Pettigrew's coat and hit the cinder path on his back. Hard. The other was hanging onto the iron hand rail outside the door. Pettigrew tried to grab hold of something with his left hand to stop his fall. There was nothing inside the door to grab hold of.

The train was moving faster, whistle screeching.

At the last second, Pettigrew's fingers gripped the door frame. It slowed his fall, but didn't keep him from pitching out onto the path. He landed on his left shoulder, and immediately rolled over onto his belly. The masked man behind him was still flat on his back. The other gave up trying to get inside the coach. He turned toward Pettigrew, and raised his pistol. The train was going past.

Pettigrew fired from where he lay, and saw the man's legs knocked from under him. He scrambled up, ran, jumped over the fallen gunman, and tried to catch the passenger coach. Legs pumping, he reached out for the iron hand rail at the coach door. He was running as fast as he had ever run in his life, but the train was still picking up speed. Desperate, teeth bared, he ran. For a second his fingers touched the rail—Only touched it. He couldn't move his feet fast enough. In a last gasping lunge he grabbed for it, missed, landed on his belly, skidded on the cinders. Skin was peeled from his face and hands.

The coach went past. Passengers' faces were pressed against the glass windows, trying to see what had happened. Cynthia's face was pressed against a window. Horrified.

All Pettigrew could do was sit on the cinder path and watch the train go. He sat there helplessly, feeling drained.

The waycar was the last. It was moving as fast as a horse could run. Soon it was far down the tracks. The steam whistle screamed.

* * *

For a long while he sat there, gasping for breath. Finally he stood. Every muscle in his body had turned to jelly. His hat lay beside the tracks, on the other side of a wounded man. The gunman, still wearing the bandana over his mouth and nose, was sitting in the cinders, holding his right thigh in both hands, groaning. On unsteady legs, Pettigrew made his way to the man, kicked his gun away, stepped over him. The other gunman was gone. Pettigrew picked up his new Stetson, noticed with a wry grin that it was no longer new, and slapped it on his head.

Voices back down the tracks drew his attention. A crowd was gathering in front of the depot. The gunfire had been heard. The town marshal, or the sheriff, or some lawman would soon join the crowd. Pettigrew didn't want to answer questions. He turned and walked as fast as his weak legs could carry him in the opposite direction.

Within a few minutes he was on the other side of a long warehouse, among stacks of new lumber. He kept going, and was soon lost in a maze of warehouses, piles of coal, stacks of bricks and empty wooden crates. Night was moving in, and soon everything had turned to vague dark shapes. A good place to disappear.

It came to him then that this was where the two gunmen had planned to disappear. When he thought about it it was easy to figure out what their plan was. They didn't intend to rob everyone in the coach. No, they knew exactly who to rob, knew what they wanted and what kind of satchel it was in. They even knew where in the coach the satchel was.

Timing was everything. Wait until the train was moving, then slip in, show their guns, grab the valise and slip out. Get out while the train was moving, but not so fast that they couldn't jump out and shoot anyone who jumped out after them. Then get over here among all this stuff and disappear in the dark.

But their timing was a shade off. They'd pulled their bandanas up too early and ruined their surprise. If they'd waited until they were inside the coach, then hid their faces and stuck a gun in Pettigrew's face, it would have worked. As it was, Pettigrew had gotten wise to them and headed them off.

So, he said to himself, I wrecked their scheme, but I wrecked my own plans too. Here I stand, knees and hands skinned from falling in the cinders, clothes dirty, while the money and the woman are hurtling north at a good thirty miles an hour.

In a voice mixed with disgust, anger and frustration, he howled his rage. "Awww shiiiit!"

Lemual Pettigrew sat in the dark on an overturned wooden crate and felt sorry for himself. He remembered vividly all he'd gone through—the bullets he'd dodged, the pain he'd endured to earn a five thousand dollars reward only to have it practically yanked out of his hands. And now he'd been shot at twice to earn half of a fifty thousand dollars ransom, and again it had been yanked right out from under him.

After he'd run it all through his mind, he began to try to figure out what to do about it. He had to get to Denver, although the woman might not be there. She'd probably keep going all the way to Chicago, where she'd have the money for herself. But he had to get to Denver and find out for sure. Hell, he had to go somewhere anyhow.

There wouldn't be another train until tomorrow evening. He could get his horse out of the livery pens and ride north to the next train stop. But he didn't care to ride all the way to Denver, so why ride at all? There was nothing to do but wait for the next train. He had money. Nearly all the eight thousand dollars that Beans Gipson had paid for the ranch was still in the money belt under his shirt. Yeah, he'd just have to wait for the next train.

Wait where?

In town he might be recognized as one of the gunmen who'd fallen out of the passenger coach. He'd be easy to recognize in his dirty clothes and skinned hands and face. He'd be pointed out to a law officer. That would end it.

Maybe he could hide out in the desert east of town until train time, then slip into the depot, buy a ticket and make himself unnoticeable in the passenger coach.

Nope. Unless he could change clothes, clean up, there was no way he could make himself inconspicuous. The town marshal, Sheriff Bowen, the deputies would all be looking for a gent who fit his description.

A long sigh came out of Pettigrew as he sat with his face in his hands and tried to think. The train was made up of one passenger coach, a string of rail cars and a waycar on the end. Some of the rail cars were gondolas loaded with coal from the mines at Trinidad. Some were flat cars loaded with lumber. Others were boxcars. The boxcars had ladders on the sides so rail-roaders could climb to the top.

Maybe — naw, it wouldn't work. Well, maybe he could stay out of sight in the desert until train time, then when the train started pulling out he could run alongside a boxcar, grab a ladder and hang on to the next stop. They wouldn't be looking for him at the next stop. There he could get in the passenger coach and buy a ticket from the conductor. He'd be noticed, that was certain, but as long as he had money he'd be sold a ticket.

Where was the next stop? Probably Colorado Springs. That was sixty or seventy miles. Three or four hours. He could hang onto a ladder that long. Or maybe climb to the top of the car.

Yeah, if he timed it right it ought to work.

Pettigrew stood and started walking. He crossed the tracks and walked east in the darkness.

Out of sight of any lights, he sat on the ground. The night was a little chilly, but the coat kept him warm. The damned thing had to be good for something. He lay on his back on a sandy spot with his hat under his head, remembering Cynthia Atkinson saying, "Waiting is awful." When daylight came he saw a line of trees farther east. A creek. Fountain Creek. That would be a better place to stay out of sight. He walked. When his stomach grumbled, he said, "Shut up," and tried his best to ignore the hollow ache in his belly.

At the creek at least he had water. A man could live a long time without eating, but not long without water. He spent the day watching birds fly from limb to limb in the cottonwoods. A brown squirrel eyed him with suspicion, sat on a limb and chattered at him, then went on about its business of rustling a living. The town was in plain view over west. There were cafes, and he had money. But on this day, he was going to have to go hungry.

At mid-afternoon the southbound went by, puffing black smoke from its smokestack, hissing, whistling. Eventually it went on south toward Trinidad. He wondered idly whether the same engine would pull a string of cars north later in the evening. No, they couldn't switch engines and unload and load cars that fast. The sun hung in the sky. Finally it was near the western horizon. Pettigrew stood, stretched and walked some of the stiffness out of his muscles. He heard the train whistle.

Fearful of being seen, he walked west toward the tracks, eyes peeled. No use trying to Indian his way. There was very little to hide behind. He walked like a man on his way to town to take care of business. Two hundred yards from the tracks he stepped down into a sandy wash. He stayed there out of sight, hoping he hadn't been noticed, waiting for the right moment. The big engine sat on the tracks, puffing and hissing. Then its whistle screeched once, twice, three times. It began to move.

Pettigrew had already picked out a boxcar four cars behind the passenger coach, three cars ahead of the waycar. It was dusk. Night was coming. He waited until the passenger car had passed, then stood up and ran. By the time he got to the tracks the train was moving at about the speed of a trotting horse. He ran, legs pumping, got hold of the iron rung of a ladder, got a good hold with both hands, then picked his feet up and groped for a foothold on the bottom rung. He was aboard. He was riding. Lord, he hoped he wasn't seen.

Just before dark, he climbed to the top of the car and found a narrow catwalk along the top. He stretched out on it, face down, holding onto the sides of it with both hands. His hat protected his face. The car swayed, rocked. The wheels clickety-clacked over the fishplates connecting the rails. Pettigrew hung on, hung on for hours.

Trying to get his mind off his predicament, he thought of Cynthia Atkinson, or whatever her last name was. Come to think of it, she'd never said. A vacation in San Francisco with her? Why not? She was beautiful, nice full soft lips, made for kissing. Full bosom, small waist, a very nice flare below the waist. The vision reminded him of how long it had been since he'd had a woman. Too damned long. A vacation with her? After all, it was her idea. Why not?

At Colorado Springs he was thankful for the darkness. He climbed down on the side opposite the depot, and walked around the end of the train. Inside, the ticket agent watched him approach, suspicious. A ticket to Denver, Pettigrew said. Can you pay for it? the agent said. His eyes widened when Pettigrew produced a roll of bills. In the men's water closet, he brushed off his clothes and hat the best he could. He washed his sore face in cold water, which got some of the dirt off but not the grime. He looked like hell.

He bought two sandwiches and got in the coach, taking an inside seat close to the door. If nobody wanted to sit next to him they sure as hell didn't have to. Nobody did. Once the train got moving again, he ate the sandwiches, then let weariness take over. He slept, using his hat for a pillow.

The sky on the eastern horizon was changing from black to a pale light when he awakened. He sat up stiffly, straightened his hat, shifted his gunbelt and

220

holster. Wouldn't be long now. What would he find?

She would be long gone, headed for Chicago. And there was nothing—not a damned thing—he could do about it. He might follow her, and he might get lucky enough to find her in the big city, but what then? She wouldn't have his twenty-five thousand dollars in her pockets, and he couldn't threaten her. She was gone. The money was gone. He was a loser. Thinking about it brought a lump to his throat, a hollowness in his chest. A loser.

Denver was such a big town that buildings appeared long before the train screeched up to the Union Depot. Tired, discouraged, dirty, Pettigrew followed other passengers through the coach door, down the iron steps, then into the huge depot. The room was crowded with people waiting for relatives, hugging relatives, shaking hands, people waiting to get on the train. He stood there, feeling lost, wondering where to start looking, wondering what to do.

And there she was.

Their eyes met halfway across the big room. He couldn't believe it. But it was the beautiful redhaired Cynthia, and she was hurrying to him, smiling.

"Lem." She was breathless. She was even more beautiful than he'd remembered. "I was so worried. I was sick with worry." She wrapped her arms around his neck and hugged him tight. He hugged her back, tried to keep his beard stubble from brushing her face.

"I'm here." That was all he could say.

She stood back at arms length, eyes searching his face, his body, smiling. "You look terrible, but we can fix that. I have a room in the Great Northern Hotel, a room for two with a private water closet. The money is in the hotel safe. We can have some food sent up. We're going to have a wonderful time now."

"A room for the two of us?" He realized he was mumbling.

"Yes. I said we are going to have a wonderful time. And that's a promise."

221

A small grin turned up one corner of Pettigrew's mouth. It spread to the other corner, then to his whole face. He smiled from ear to ear.

"I hear you talking," he said.